HARBOR CODE

HARBOR CODE

Talk of The Town Series
Book Two

Parker Daugherty

Underfoot Press
Oakland, California

First published in 2026 by Underfoot Press
Oakland, California
www.underfootpress.com

Talk of The Town Series
Book Two

Copyediting by Olivia M. Ward
Cover design by Parker Daugherty

First edition

ISBN: 979-8-950967-01-6

Printed in the United States of America

10 9 8 7 6 5 4 3 2 1

For the readers who stayed,
the friends who said keep going,
and everyone who found a piece of home in these pages.

For those who love the Bay Area,
and for those who simply love someone who does.

I'll keep talking about The Town.
Count on it.

Talk of The Town Series

Book One — Brass Secrets

Book Two — Harbor Code

Book Three — Hall of Frame

Book Four — Past & Perfect

Contents

Key Location in Harbor Code

PROLOGUE

Beacon

* * *

BEACON — signal light used to guide vessels through darkness or danger.

* * *

Port of Oakland: Late Night

The cranes loomed like skeletons against the night sky, steel arms frozen mid-gesture. Below them, the docks churned with motion: forklifts whining, the thud of containers settling on concrete, headlamps slicing through fog that rolled off the Bay. The air was heavy with salt, diesel, and cold iron.

Near the perimeter of the secured yard—close enough to blend, far enough to avoid attention—a container sat temporarily staged for transfer. Its seal had been scanned, logged, and cleared.

Nothing about it suggested urgency.

A crew moved with practiced efficiency. Reflective vests. Hard hats. Badge clips catching light. They looked like every other shift on the dock.

Inside the container, crates gleamed under thin beams of light. One by one, the men slid them down a ramp into waiting box trucks, paperwork clipped neatly to dashboards. Engines idled low, patient.

Three hundred feet beyond the fencing, where the industrial lights thinned into shadow, a black sedan waited with its engine running.

In the rear seat, a woman leaned forward, binoculars pressed to her eyes. A belted peacoat cinched her waist, the wool a deep charcoal that swallowed light. Knee-high boots crossed at the ankle. A wide-brimmed hat with fur trim shadowed her face just enough to make features indistinct. Black gloves lay folded beside her like punctuation.

She lifted her phone, voice cool but resonant. "Status."

From the yard, a man's voice answered, breath steady. "First truck sealed. Second loading now."

"How many crates remain?"

A pause. Counting. "Nine."

"And the gate?"

"Clear."

"Good."

She ended the call and adjusted her glove, smoothing the leather along each finger before slipping it back on.

At the container, another man stood beside a vehicle that did not belong to the port. A laptop rested on the hood. His fingers moved quickly, confidently.

A digital record flickered, re-routed, reconciled, then vanished.

Tomorrow there would be one fewer container than had ever been logged.

Tonight, the cranes still moved. The ships still docked. Oakland's heartbeat thudded on as though nothing had shifted.

The trucks rolled out in staggered intervals, taillights fading toward a warehouse in West Oakland that would not appear on any official routing manifest.

The woman in the peacoat did not lean back.

She watched until the last truck cleared the gate.

Then she folded her arms, a flash of gold at her wrist catching the dashboard light.

Phase one was complete.

The real work hadn't even begun.

PART I

CHAPTER ONE

The Keel

* * *

KEEL — structural backbone of a vessel.

* * *

Port of Oakland: Morning

Thomas Forrester stood at the loading bay, clipboard tucked under one arm, watching a flatbed ease toward Berth 22. The shipment had arrived under seal from Indonesia, flagged for inspection by the U.S. Fish and Wildlife Service—one of the few kinds of cargo that still made crews uneasy. The labels read *Live Specimens* and *Fragile*, and rumor said the crates held birds or reptiles bound for quarantine at the Oakland Zoo.

"Easy now," he called to the driver as the forklift lurched forward. "Slow and square. Put her down gently."

The driver, young and showing off, grinned through the windshield and gunned the throttle. The forks clipped a brace. The entire pallet shuddered, and a deep metallic crack echoed across the yard.

"Kill the engine!" Thomas barked.

Too late. The corner of the container crumpled with a groan. For a heartbeat everyone froze. Then horns blared, men scattered, and curses cut through the yard. A federal inspector threw up a hand, signaling for distance.

Thomas ran in. "Back it up, Ray, and lock the wheels," he ordered, grabbing the emergency straps. Mist poured from the cracked seal, followed by a faint rustle—something alive inside.

"Nobody touches a thing until Fish and Wildlife clears it."

By the time calm returned, a section of the yard was taped off and a federal officer was already taking statements from the stevedores.

Field Officer Clare Hinton, U.S. Fish and Wildlife.

Quick eyes. Hair pulled tight. Clipboard clutched like armor.

She moved through the scene with quiet efficiency, checking seals, asking questions, and directing the containment crew.

Twice Thomas looked up to find her watching him.

When he turned and met her eyes, she looked away first.

When he looked again, she was gone.

Hours later, in the office above the yard, Thomas finished his report:

Operator negligence — no injuries — container integrity compromised — cargo transferred under supervision of U.S. FWS.

Thirty years on the job, and the paperwork never ended. He signed his name and exhaled.

When he came down, the crew was already swapping stories—half amusement, half frustration. He didn't add to it.

"Accidents happen," he said. "We clean them up and move on."

But as he left the yard, he noticed how many men stopped talking when he passed.

He could sense the shift.

He told himself it was the contract tension. Nothing more.

* * *

Inside the longshore workers' breakroom, the coffee on the burner had gone bitter. Salt still clung to jackets draped over hooks. Fluorescent lights buzzed overhead as two representatives of the International Longshore and Warehouse Union (ILWU) sat hunched over a scarred table, voices pitched low but tight with frustration.

"I'm telling you, management isn't budging," one said, rubbing his temples. "Shift caps, real healthcare, wages that don't cover rent—they just shake their heads."

"They're stalling," the other growled. "But this port doesn't run without us. The cranes don't move unless we say so."

"They'll remember soon enough," the first muttered. "The contract's about to expire. If we pull the line, every ship sits. Trucks, trains—the whole West Coast freezes overnight."

"Good," the second snapped. "Maybe it's time they felt it."

Thomas Forrester had heard enough before he stepped inside to know where the conversation was headed.

He took in the room with a calm nod.

"You're not wrong to be angry," he said. "But that's why we have contracts. That's why labor and management bargain at the table—to make sure it's a fair deal. The process isn't over yet."

One man frowned. The other gave a slow nod.

Thomas poured himself a cup of coffee, the pot sputtering on the burner.

"We fight if we have to," he added, "but we don't jump the gun. The dockers built this city once—we don't burn it down out of frustration."

The older of the two sighed. "You're right, Forrester. You've been through more of these rounds than any of us. But if they keep stonewalling, something's going to break."

Thomas stirred his coffee, the spoon clinking against the chipped mug.

"Then let it break at the table," he said quietly. "That's where we win—not out there in the cold."

Neither man noticed the younger dockworker sweeping near the doorway. He moved slowly, broom rasping across the concrete, a faded A's cap shadowing his eyes.

When the reps finally rose and left, the sweeper paused, thumbed a quick text, hit **SEND**, and slipped the phone back into his pocket before the screen went dark.

CHAPTER TWO

Crosscurrents

* * *

CROSSCURRENTS — opposing flows of water.

* * *

The kitchen smelled of garlic and simmering tomatoes when Maya slipped onto the stool at the counter. Her mother, Doris, moved with practiced ease, apron tied at the waist, wooden spoon in hand as she stirred the sauce.

"You've got good timing," Doris said without looking up. "I just put the lasagna in. I know it's both you and your grandfather's favorite."

Maya smiled, chin propped in her hand.

"You mean *Skipper*?"

Doris chuckled. "He'll always be Skipper to you. To me, he was just the father who vanished for months and came back barking orders like we were crew."

Her voice softened as she turned back to the sauce.

"That's partly why I worked at the Naval Supply Center when I was your age. It felt like my way of staying close to him, even if he wasn't home. I was a keypunch operator back then.

Maya leaned forward, listening.

"It sounds like you were basically tracking containers before computers made it easy."

"Exactly." Doris tapped her spoon against the pot.

She plated some cheese, crackers, and fruit and set it in front of Maya, pouring sparkling water into two stemless flutes. The fizz caught the kitchen light like scattered glass.

Doris leaned her hip against the counter, watching her daughter with that mix of pride and scrutiny only a mother could manage.

Her tone shifted, warmer but edged with worry.

"Maya, you've got your grandfather's nose for detail. But are you using it? From what I hear you say, you can do your job in your sleep. Is that really enough for you?"

Maya smiled faintly, breaking a cracker in half.

"Since when did being good at something turn into a crime?"

"That's not what I meant." Doris sat across from her, folding her hands. "You're good at what you do because you don't miss things. But lately I get the feeling you're... coasting."

"You were never the type to settle for checking boxes."

"I'm not coasting. I'm—"

Maya hesitated, searching for a word that didn't sound like an excuse.

"—comfortable."

Doris arched an eyebrow.

"Comfort's fine if it fills you. But you look restless. Your father says you've been asking a lot of questions about the port."

"Maybe I just like knowing what's going on."

"Or maybe you're looking for something more."

Doris's voice softened.

"Your grandfather used to say some people see the world as it is, and others see the patterns underneath. You were always one of the latter. Even as a kid, you couldn't leave a puzzle alone."

Maya traced a circle on the condensation of her glass.

Doris's smile was gentle but knowing.

"Just promise me you'll remember curiosity can be a door... and sometimes a trap."

Maya met her mother's eyes, hearing the unspoken worry beneath the advice.

"I know, Mom. I'm just... tired of watching other people make all the choices. If there's something wrong out there, I want to understand it."

Doris studied her for a long moment.

The front door opened with a rush of cool air.

Maya's father stepped in first, windbreaker zipped from the drive. Behind him, Captain Byron "Harp" Harper entered with his overnight bag slung casually over his shoulder, posture as straight as if he'd just stepped off a ship's deck.

Maya was up in an instant, throwing her arms around him. "Skipper."

He squeezed her back, grinning.

"I remember when you were a baby and called me *Skippy*. Couldn't get enough of it. Still the best promotion I ever had."

Maya laughed, pulling back to look at him.

"You'll always be Skipper to me."

He set down his bag and sniffed the air.

"Smells like my daughter hasn't lost her touch."

Doris rolled her eyes with a smile. "Thirty years at sea and you still call me your daughter like it's a rank."

Dinner began warmly, with easy stories: Harp recalling the first time he brought Maya aboard a ship for Fleet Week, Thomas adding a tale from the yard, Doris teasing them both about their stubborn streaks.

But the mood shifted when the talk edged toward the coming week.

Thomas set his fork down, voice measured but firm.

"The contract's at the breaking point. If management doesn't move, we'll strike for sure. Once the cranes stop, the ships wait. It'll send a message."

Harp's brow furrowed.

"During Fleet Week? When the Navy comes to honor its service members? That's when you want to shut down the port?"

"It's not about Fleet Week," Thomas said. "It's about respect. My men risk their lives every shift. They deserve fair contracts, not excuses."

Doris leaned in, siding with her husband.

"It's not about showmanship, Dad. It's about survival. Healthcare, safety and living wages."

Harp stabbed at his food, jaw tight.

"Strikes don't fix broken systems. They make civilians look reckless. And it dishonors the Navy's presence here."

Maya spoke carefully, bridging the silence.

"Maybe it shows both," Maya said, "the Navy's strength and the workers' power."

"The whole coast, Tacoma to San Diego, runs because longshore workers show up every day, moving what the country needs," she continued. "That's worth respecting. That's worth fighting for."

The table fell quiet, each holding their ground, waiting for someone to decide which way they would move.

Skipper drew a slow breath, rubbing the back of his neck.

When he finally spoke, his voice had lost its edge.

"You're right, May. Maybe I was thinking too small."

"Fleet Week comes and goes. The work your father and his union do—that's what keeps food on tables, fuel in tanks, ships moving. Including mine."

He glanced at Thomas, then back at Maya, his expression softer.

"Didn't mean to sound like a kid wanting fireworks while the grown-ups hold the line."

"You made your point."

"And it's a damn good one."

CHAPTER THREE

The Lookout

* * *

Lookout — crew member assigned to watch the sea.

* * *

Across town, the water ran on the highest, hottest setting for a full minute before Clare adjusted the handle a quarter turn cooler. Steam swelled until her glasses fogged. She abandoned them on the shelf. Here in the pounding roar, her mind finally quieted.

She thought about the crime series she had binged the night before, the ones where investigators always said the truth lived in the smallest details.

The heat built, and she let it. She even turned the hot water up a little more as her body acclimated. The water drummed her shoulders, neck and back until they burned, and still she stayed beneath it, trying to see through the fog in her head.

She replayed the scene again, slowing each moment in her mind. The forklift driver grinning, turning too fast. The crack of metal against concrete. The longshoreman yelling. One, the lead, grabbing the emergency straps. Forrester. His name was in her report.

She twisted off the water, wrapped a towel around herself, and padded barefoot through the apartment.

Port inspections were usually routine. This one had not been. Forrester was as good as they came. He had an answer ready for every question in the report.

She turned toward the kitchen, unaware of the faint wet footprints she left trailing down the hall.

She ran her fingers through her wet hair and shook it, letting the water droplets fly. The tension she felt was familiar. Was it one too many crime shows or something else?

* * *

Four thousand seven hundred twenty-five steps from trailhead to Point Arnold. From the public overlook at Middle Harbor, the Port of Oakland unfolded in long, measured lines.

The wind pressed hard off the Bay. Slate jacket zipped to the chin. Gloves snug at the wrist. Doc Martens firm against the grated steps of the observation tower. The brass key at her throat shifted once as she leaned forward.

Steel cranes rose and fell with mechanical patience. Trucks queued at the gates in slow procession. Tugboats eased vessels into position like hands guiding something too large to turn itself.

To most people, it was industry.

To her, it was structure.

She had not come here by accident.

Three nights earlier, she had followed a familiar sedan as it slipped toward the industrial corridor along Maritime Street. It had not entered the yard. It had not lingered. It had simply been present—close enough to matter, far enough to avoid notice.

That was enough.

She walked the same two miles each morning now. Four thousand seven hundred twenty-five steps. She counted because repetition steadied the mind.

Repetition made change visible.

She lifted the public binoculars.

She watched the routine.

Shift changes. Gate cycles. Inspection lanes.

A never-ending rhythm of movement.

She wrote times in a small notebook. Arrival windows. Departure clusters. Which berths turned over faster than others.

She did not yet know what she was looking for.

Only that if something was happening, it would eventually disturb the rhythm.

Below her, trucks moved in measured intervals. Nothing rushed. Nothing stalled.

For now.

She lowered the binoculars and stepped back from the rail, scanning the empty path behind her before descending the stairs.

She had learned the hard way that waiting for proof was often too late.

For now, instinct would have to be enough.

Tomorrow she would walk the same four thousand seven hundred twenty-five steps.

She would stand here again.

And that was reason enough to learn how it worked.

Come hell.

Or high water.

CHAPTER FOUR

First Watch

* * *

FIRST WATCH — the first shift standing guard.

* * *

The bells of Mills Hall tolled across the Oakland campus, their sound carrying through the eucalyptus groves and down toward the meadow where rows of folding chairs faced a stage draped in blue and gold.

Fiona Lynette Phillips adjusted the edge of her mortarboard, re-pinning it to her braided ponytail. She gripped the folded speech in her hand.

Valedictorian.

The word still felt unreal.

When her name was called, the applause rose first from the student section, then from scattered families waving programs and hand-painted signs. Fiona climbed the steps to the podium, her dark gown swaying in the warm June air, and paused a moment to steady herself.

"Good afternoon," she began, her voice carrying through the speakers. "We are standing at the threshold between two worlds. Behind us, years of study, of questions that turned into better questions, of nights spent writing papers that mattered only because they made us think harder about the kind of people we want to become. Ahead of us, a city, a country, a world that desperately needs us to carry that same questioning spirit into every space we enter."

She looked out at the crowd—professors, parents, neighbors, and friends.

"For me, literary studies were never about books on a shelf. It was about people. The stories they tell, the stories they're denied, and the courage it takes to speak when silence is easier. Critical theory taught me that justice begins with listening, and with refusing to let someone else write your story for you."

Fiona let the pause linger, then smiled.

"So today, we leave this campus not just with degrees, but with responsibility. To ask better questions. To keep listening. To demand a world where stories aren't erased, but preserved, remembered, and told. That is our work, and it doesn't end here."

The audience rose in applause, the sound rolling like thunder beneath the grove.

As Fiona stepped back from the podium, she caught sight of three familiar figures near the back of the crowd.

Ben whooped loud enough to draw a few amused looks from nearby faculty, pumping his fist in the air. Beside him, Maya bounced on her toes, clapping above her head with unrestrained joy while Rich tried to keep his camera steady and trained on the podium, laughing as he captured the moment through his lens.

Their cheers rose above the rest, and Fiona's grin widened until it ached.

* * *

Later, the four of them gathered around a table crowded with empty plates and half-finished glasses.

Late afternoon sunlight shimmered across Lake Merritt, the ripples throwing gold against the shaded dock of the restaurant. For once, Fiona wasn't carrying trays or checking tabs.

She was the one being served.

Rich slipped an arm along the back of Maya's chair as he scrolled through the photos on his camera.

"Got it," he said. "The exact moment Ben embarrassed himself."

"Worth it," Ben replied immediately.

Her former coworkers emerged from the kitchen with wide grins, balancing a cake layered in frosting and decorated with a scrawl of chocolate: **Congratulations, Fiona!**

The table erupted in cheers as the servers set it down, laughing and clapping her on the shoulder before drifting back inside.

Maya pulled Fiona's diploma from its envelope and held it up like a prize while Rich leaned in to photograph it.

"Fiona Lynette Phillips," she announced proudly, "Master of Arts in Literary Studies with a focus on social justice and critical theory."

She reached across the table and squeezed Fiona's hand.

"You did it," she said softly.

Rich leaned across the table, his grin irrepressible.

"Super proud of you, Fi. Not just for getting through it—but for making it look easy. Congratulations."

Fiona flushed, shaking her head, though her eyes were bright.

Ben lifted his glass, the setting sun catching the amber liquid inside.

"To Fiona," he said. "To her words, her courage, and the future she's going to shape."

He glanced around the table, smiling.

"And may we be lucky enough to be a part of it."

They raised their glasses together, the clink sharp and clear against the hum of the lakefront.

CHAPTER FIVE

The Ballast

* * *

BALLAST — weight placed in a vessel to improve stability.

* * *

Weeks later, Maya and Fiona jogged side by side along the Embarcadero, sneakers slapping the pavement in rhythm. The fog still clung low over the Bay, softening the line between the water and the cranes that loomed faintly in the distance.

They slowed near the marina, catching their breath. A bright poster flapped against a lamppost: Fleet Week – October 2007. Parade of Ships. Blue Angels Air Show.

Fiona grinned, tugging her earbuds down. "Hard to believe it's that time again. Do you ever go?" she jutted her chin towards the poster.

Maya brushed a stray curl back, eyes lingering on the image of the USS Bonhomme Richard under the Golden Gate. "Yes, every year when I was growing up. My grandpa used to take me. He'd come up from San Diego every October. We made a whole ritual out of it. We'd take the ship tours, watch the Blue Angels, and enjoy the street food. We did everything together."

"Is he coming again this year?" Fiona asked.

Maya's smile widened. "He's already here. He's being honored for thirty years of service as a captain in the Navy. The whole family's planning to celebrate. You and Ben will get invites too."

"Trust me," Maya added with a laugh, "Grandpa still has a sea story for every ship in the fleet. Half the time he'd teach me semaphore on the pier just to prove a point."

Fiona shook her head, smiling. "That sounds wonderful. And I'm not saying no to that invitation."

Above them, a distant roar split the sky. They looked up as a pair of jets streaked overhead, contrails carving bright arcs through the thinning fog.

Fiona shaded her eyes. "Your grandpa's going to love that."

"He will," Maya said softly. "He always does."

"Fiona, you know that Rich and I will be in court when Ben testifies right?" Maya searched her face.

"Yes, we expected that."

Uncle Wallace is coming too.

"Ben needs everyone's support. He is a little nervous."

"Well, that's reasonable, given everything he went through, that we went through." Maya folded her arms and shifted her weight. "Tell him not to worry. Right is right, and Ellsworth is going to pay for his crimes."

“That’s the plan, for sure.” Fiona crossed her fingers on both hands and held both hands up, grinning.

At home, Maya wiped a nonexistent ring from the counter and smiled. Clean lines, everything in its place. She preferred order and she could control that easily in her home.

Her phone chimed. A text: Over and Out, from Rich, his way of saying he was heading home. She texted back the same phrase, their private echo.

* * *

That night, Maya's laptop hummed while the evening news ran like background static. Rows of numbers filled her monitor, formulas stacking until patterns emerged.

The anchor's voice drifted over her shoulder: "...the high-profile corruption case of Paul Ellsworth enters its final phase this week. Jury selection has concluded, and opening arguments begin tomorrow morning in Alameda County Superior Court..."

She rubbed her eyes, leaning back. Ellsworth. The name still felt sharp even through the neutral cadence of the newscaster.

The key rattled in the lock. Rich shouldered the door open, a bag of takeout dangling from one hand. "Normal people unwind with TV, not spreadsheets," he said, setting the bag on the counter.

Maya muted the broadcast but kept her gaze on the screen, where a photo of Ellsworth in his power-broker days glowed beside the anchor's head. "The trial starts tomorrow."

Rich unpacked cartons, stacking them neatly. “Strange, seeing Ellsworth dragged into court after everything the four of us went through with him. And with Ben as the star witness, I hope he's ready for that kind of spotlight."

"I saw Fiona," Maya said. "She said he's nervous but ready."

"He doesn't have a choice," Rich replied quietly. "Ellsworth has a lot to answer for. For Ben, this is a chance to set the record straight."

He slid chopsticks across the table toward her.

For a moment the apartment felt smaller, the hum of the refrigerator louder, Ellsworth's smirk frozen on the muted TV.

The reporters kept saying tomorrow the city gets closure. She wasn't so sure. Tonight, the memories pressed close, unspoken but alive.

Maya rubbed her eyes and checked the clock. Tomorrow Ben would stand in a room full of cameras and try to make the truth hold.

CHAPTER SIX

Shadow Waters

* * *

SHADOW WATERS — visibility is uncertain and depth is unclear.

* * *

Across town, Ben Cooper sat at his kitchen table with a stack of files spread before him. His father's old leather journal rested open at his side, its worn edges and faded initials grounding him.

He read through his notes one more time. Every line carried the weight of broken promises and stolen neighborhoods.

He closed the file and pressed his palms flat against the wood, steadying his breath. The thought of facing Paul Ellsworth in court quickened his pulse, but he did not flinch.

The corridor outside the courtroom smelled faintly of polish and paper, the kind of air that clung to government buildings. Reporters clustered near the doors, notebooks ready, cameras hanging low at their sides.

Ben stood with Rich, Maya, Fiona, and Wallace in a tight circle near the wall. He adjusted the cuffs of his shirt and straightened his tie.

"You've got this," Fiona said, her voice warm but firm. "Just tell the truth."

Ben's uncle Wallace set a steady hand on his shoulder. "You know those records better than anyone. You did the work when others wouldn't."

"Trust that. Trust yourself."

Maya offered a small smile. "You're not standing up there alone. You've got all of us with you."

A man with a union patch on his jacket slowed as he walked past the group.

"I recognize you. You're Ben Cooper, right? Good luck. You're speaking for all of us."

An older woman pressed a hand to his arm. "You've already done more than anyone could have asked. Whatever happens, we're proud of you."

Ben nodded, the weight of their eyes heavy but steadying. "Thank you. I'll do my best."

The bailiff's voice carried down the hall.

"Court is now in session."

Alameda County Superior Court brimmed with bodies. Wooden benches creaked beneath citizens, activists, journalists, and city employees.

Light slanted through high windows, dust motes drifting in the air. The hush was thick, broken only by the rustle of papers and the shuffle of shoes against the tiled floor.

The bailiff called out, "Superior Court of California, County of Alameda. The People versus Paul Ellsworth. All rise."

The door to her chambers opened. In walked the judge, her black robe pressed and immaculate.

She wore her hair natural, a soft halo of coils framing her face. Thin rectangular glasses rested low on her nose. Behind the lenses her eyes were sharp and discerning.

She took her seat without a word.

The courtroom rumbled as everyone settled back into their seats. Maya studied the judge carefully.

Paul Ellsworth sat at the defense table, silver cufflinks gleaming against his pressed suit. He looked thinner than the photos from his power-broker days, but the table around him told another story.

A row of high-priced attorneys flanked him, their briefcases lined up like sentries—each a reminder that Ellsworth never fought his battles alone.

His smirk held, but his fingers brushed the edge of a legal pad twice before he stilled them, a sheen of sweat already rising at his temple.

The district attorney rose from his seat, steady and precise.

"Ladies and gentlemen of the jury, you will hear how the defendant siphoned redevelopment funds, falsified contracts, and betrayed the trust of Oakland's citizens. This was deliberate theft, not oversight."

Ellsworth's attorney countered smoothly, pacing before the jury box.

"The prosecution has assembled half-truths and conjecture—bitter testimony twisted into a story. But Mr.

Ellsworth is no criminal. His efforts brought investment to this city."

Ben raised his right hand, his voice steady as the oath echoed through the chamber.

The microphones caught every syllable. The crowd hushed, waiting. Papers rustled, camera shutters clicked.

He thought of his father's words—records are the backbone of a city—and let the sentence anchor him.

The weight of the room shifted toward him.

CHAPTER SEVEN

The Lighthouse

* * *

LIGHTHOUSE — a tower casting light across dangerous water.

* * *

When Ben spoke, his voice carried clean and certain, though Maya heard the strain beneath it—the cost of standing there alone.

The judge leaned forward, her expression unreadable. Maya's pulse matched the tick of the wall clock. For a moment she imagined the whole city holding its breath.

It wasn't just him on trial; it was everything he represented.

Ellsworth shifted at the defense table. Maya felt heat rise behind her ribs.

"Mr. Cooper, how familiar are you with the redevelopment projects attributed to Paul Ellsworth?"

Maya exhaled softly. It was the setup she expected. Ben was on solid ground.

Ben cleared his throat.

"I worked in the city planning division, overseeing contracts, timelines, and public records tied to redevelopment projects."

The district attorney nodded.

"And why are you testifying today?"

Maya felt her head nodding, as if the questions were meant for her instead of Ben.

Ben paused. Then he raised his chin just slightly, and his voice carried easily across the expanse of the courtroom.

"The only reason I can even say this today is because my father and others like him fought to protect those records. Ellsworth tried to erase that truth, to bend it to his advantage. But the evidence remained."

Maya felt her hands tighten into fists as Ben's final words pushed past the objections of Ellsworth's attorneys.

"Paul Ellsworth is not a builder. He is a liar and a cheat. Men like him—who put power over people—are the reason this city still struggles."

Murmurs rippled through the gallery until the judge's gavel snapped the room back to silence.

On cross-examination, Ellsworth's attorney rose smoothly.

"Mr. Cooper, you once worked in city planning, but you lost your job. Is that why you are here testifying today? Because you are bitter about losing your position?"

The nerve of him.

Maya leaned back, crossing her arms.

Ben's voice stayed firm.

"If I had failed at my job, I would have walked away quietly. I didn't fail. I found the truth."

A ripple of applause broke out in the gallery before the judge's gavel slammed it down again.

But the words lingered.

* * *

That night the city seemed to hold its breath. Maya sat at her kitchen table with the television muted, the glow from the news crawl flickering against the glass.

Ben had spoken for all of them, she thought. He had done everything right, and still she couldn't shake the feeling that words alone might not be enough.

* * *

It was crowded at Key and Cup, the café co-owned by Ben and Fiona, the day the verdict came in.

The café had gone quiet without anyone noticing when it happened. Even the espresso machine had fallen silent.

Fiona stood behind the counter with her arms folded. Wallace leaned forward in his chair.

Ben didn't sit. He just watched the screen.

The anchor looked up.

"We are receiving word now from Alameda County Superior Court..."

Uncle Wallace rubbed his hands together slowly.

"Whatever happens," he said quietly, "that man has to answer for something."

The words hung in the air.

The camera cut to the courtroom as the jury foreman was asked to stand and read the verdict.

"We the jury, find Paul R. Ellsworth, not guilty..."

A chyron scrolled across the screen:

ELLSWORTH AVOIDS PRISON – COMMUNITY SERVICE, FINES

The news hit like cold water.

No one spoke.

Ellsworth adjusted his cufflinks, then turned toward the cameras, smiling as though nothing had touched him.

Fiona switched off the sound. The silence was heavier than the noise.

"Community service?" Fiona muttered, slamming her mug down.

Wallace shook his head. "That's what you give a kid tagging walls, not a man who stole millions."

At a nearby table, a woman shook her head.

"He stole from us. And they still let him walk."

Another voice cut in, younger and sharp.

"He wasn't totally vindicated. They found him not guilty of the most severe charges but he's still going to pay something. Anyway, it doesn't matter. He's just one man. But people are paying attention now. Even me, I just registered to vote last week for the first time."

Fiona leaned over, seizing the thread.

"Good. Keep telling your friends. I'm hosting sign-ups here every Saturday. If the system won't protect us, then we must use the ballots we have to change it."

A man near the door nodded toward Ben.

"You should keep talking like you did in that courtroom. People listen."

Maya stared at the screen, her voice tight with fury.

"He walked out smiling. Like it was all a game."

Rich barked a bitter laugh.

"Guess crime does pay, if you've got the right legal team."

Maya shook her head, eyes still fixed on the footage.

"If this is how the system works, that's not justice."

The words hung there heavier than she meant, and she pressed her lips together.

Rich saw the seriousness in her face and heard the steel in her voice.

Ben stood apart, his mug cooling in his hands, the replay flickering across the screen.

Ellsworth strolled past the cameras, waving as if leaving a parade instead of a courtroom.

CHAPTER EIGHT

Bearing Lines

* * *

BEARING LINES — line used to determine position.

* * *

Two days after the verdict, Maya sat at her desk pretending to work. Her screen glowed, numbers stacking into neat patterns she no longer cared about. Formulas aligned, graphs rendered clean, but lately they felt like wallpaper, tidy and meaningless.

She barely registered the broadcast until the anchor's tone sharpened:

"...The International Longshore and Warehouse Union (ILWU), which controls nearly every major container port on the Pacific seaboard from Los Angeles to Seattle, confirmed its members will walk out if talks collapse. Analysts warn that when ILWU workers stop, cargo bottlenecks ripple through the entire West Coast supply chain."

Her pen hovered, the word *strike* already underlined twice in her notebook.

On the muted screen, the crawl replayed a clip of Paul Ellsworth striding out of court the day before, waving to cameras with that smug grin. He'd stolen millions, been exposed, and still walked free.

Maya swallowed hard.

One more broken promise of justice. One more reminder that the rules bent for men like him.

The apartment door rattled open. Rich stepped inside, cheeks flushed from his run, sweatshirt damp at the collar.

In his hands was a warm paper sack fragrant with grilled meat and cilantro.

"Stopped by the taco truck," he said, dropping it onto the counter. "Got your favorites. Figured I earned it after running those stairs twice."

Maya muted the television, her eyes still fixed on the crawl of text.

"A strike is looking more certain by the day," she murmured, circling the word again.

Rich pulled out the cartons. "Let's just have dinner in peace and leave the world outside for now."

"This is big," Maya said. "It's serious."

He glanced over at her, a tortilla chip paused halfway to his mouth. His tone softened, more concerned than mocking.

"Maya... don't you have enough on your plate? Why are you so worried about this strike?"

She set her pen down, meeting his eyes.

"I stare at data all day, Rich. My dad spends his life under those cranes. Right now my work feels like noise. This matters." she gestured at the screen, "real lives are being impacted."

Rich frowned, though not unkindly. "You're good at what you do. You've built a career..."

"And maybe it's the wrong one," she interjected.

"Maya, this isn't yours to solve. Ben had his fight with Ellsworth. That was one thing. But a port strike? That's dangerous ground."

"Well, it concerned you when Ben asked for your support," she shot back. "You didn't hesitate then."

The chip lowered slowly. Rich studied her face now, eyes narrowing.

"You're right," he said finally. "Ben needed someone in his corner. Apparently I need to do a better job of listening."

Maya's voice softened, but her resolve held.

"Yes. It does. I don't want to keep living like I'm passing time between workdays. If my dad's union is being pushed into a corner, I can't look away."

Rich leaned closer, setting the chips aside.

"Then talk to me. What's your plan?"

She exhaled, tension easing when she saw him lean in.

"I'm meeting my dad for coffee. I'll start there."

Rich nodded. "Good. Ask the questions you need to ask. Just... keep it to fact-finding."

"I promise," she said quietly.

A beat passed. The air was warmer now, less sharp.

Rich's grin returned.

"But after coffee with your dad, we're overdue for a night out. Just us. Candles, menus, the works."

Maya's reluctant smile tugged at her lips.

"Okay. Coffee with Dad, and dinner with you."

"Now that's a deal I'll take."

* * *

The next day, Maya slid into a booth across from her father at a café in Jack London Square.

Thomas Forrester still wore his yard vest, the reflective stripes dulled by dust. His boots were scuffed, his hands rough—the kind that told their own history. He set his coffee down with the precision of a man who never wasted motion.

"You've heard about the contract negotiations," he said.

Not a question.

Maya nodded, pen poised above her notebook.

"Yes. Is the process deadlocked?"

"Management says no money. We say no deal." His voice cut like steel on steel. "If the contract expires without a fix, the cranes stop moving. Ships sit at anchor, trucks idle at the gates, trains stay cold. A strike shuts the whole line down."

Maya glanced past his shoulder, across the water to San Francisco's glittering shoreline.

"I thought San Francisco used to run the ports?"

Thomas followed her gaze, a dry smile tugging at his mouth.

"Before the container ships, back in the day, San Francisco was where all the work was for longshoremen. But those old finger piers couldn't take the big ships. Too shallow, too cramped. By the seventies it was done. The work came over here. Oakland had deep water, railways, and room for cranes. That's why the whole coast leans on us now."

She turned back, the cranes outside shifting in her eyes—no longer silent machinery but something alive. Something that could stop whenever her father and his men decided.

Thomas wrapped his calloused fingers around the mug again, steam curling against his jaw. His voice lowered, blunt but unwavering.

"If it comes to a strike, May, the city will feel it. Every family, every street. That's the weight of it."

He hesitated, then exhaled, his shoulders easing back against the booth.

"But there's something else," he said quietly. "Something I can't quite put my finger on."

Maya's pen stilled above her notebook.

"What do you mean?"

Thomas's eyes shifted to the window, following a truck rolling along the edge of the pier.

"There've been runs at odd hours. Trucks coming and going when the gates are supposed to be locked."

"I've been at that yard longer than some of those supervisors have been alive. You learn the rhythms. The sound of the cranes, the timing of the lights, the way the air shifts when something's off."

He tapped the table once.

"And this... this is off."

Maya frowned. "Have you reported it?"

“I did. Management said they’d beef up security.” He gave a humorless chuckle. “If security’s part of the problem, that won’t fix much.”

“Part of the problem?”

“Money, May.” He sighed, running a hand over his jaw. “Always comes down to money. Some guards looking for a little extra. A foreman trying to make his mortgage. A kid in his first year thinking a side deal might help with daycare or debt.”

“It doesn’t take much. Good people start convincing themselves it’s harmless—just moving a crate or two. Then one day they’ve lost the job, the pension, the respect that took decades to earn.”

She read his face as he spoke, noticing the deep lines at the corners of his eyes, the quiet resignation beneath his words.

“I wish I was wrong,” he said finally. “But I’ve seen this movie before. First come the whispers, then somebody gets caught holding the bag. Always the ones at the bottom who pay.”

Maya closed her notebook.

“You’re worried, aren’t you?”

“I am,” he said quietly. “If the strike hits, the whole mess will get buried under the noise.”

They sat in silence for a moment, the cranes outside still turning slowly against the brightening sky.

Maya reached across the table, brushing her fingers lightly against the back of his hand.

“You’ve kept the port running your whole career, Dad. If something’s happening, someone needs to see it for what it is.”

He looked at her, half proud, half weary.

She smiled faintly.

"Then it's a good thing they have you. I'm just… trying to understand it."

CHAPTER NINE

The Channel

* * *

CHANNEL — path of safe water through hazards

* * *

The drive stretched long and empty and Maya kept the radio low, half listening to a call-in show about the pending strike. Every voice sounded the same; tired, angry, waiting for someone else to fix it.

Her father's words lingered in her head.

Trucks coming and going at odd hours. No manifests. Management promising tighter security.

He'd said it like a man reporting bad weather, like it was inevitable but still disappointing.

And then, softer:

Good men can get stupid when fast money starts talking.

She gripped the wheel tighter. He'd sounded resigned, but she wasn't. The thought of the docks turning into another scheme, another place where rules bent for profit, made her stomach twist.

A sign flashed past for her exit.

Instead of turning toward home, she stayed on the road toward the Oakland hills.

She wasn't sure why until the thought formed.

Ellsworth.

The name still soured her mouth. The papers had called his sentence a chance for rehabilitation. She called it a farce. Restitution, fines, community service—barely a slap on the wrist for a man who'd drained whole neighborhoods.

The streets wound upward into quiet affluence. The estates were manicured and silent, the kind of wealth that hid behind hedges and keypad gates.

Instead of envy, she felt irritation.

He still lived here. Of course he did.

Men like Paul Ellsworth didn't fall. They just built shorter ladders to climb again.

She pulled to the curb a block from his gate.

The house glowed behind wrought iron, warm and untouched. A figure moved past a window—jacket pressed, movements precise.

Minutes later, the gates slid open and the black sedan rolled out.

Her pulse quickened.

She told herself it was curiosity, but when her headlights caught his taillights, she matched his speed.

She wanted to see where power went when the courtroom lights went out.

He drove toward the waterfront, the city's neon reflecting off wet asphalt. By the time he reached Jack London Square, the streets had thinned to bars closing early and trucks idling by the tracks.

He turned down a narrow alley and stopped beneath a flickering pink sign.

The Pink Lady.

From the street it passed for an old jazz club—the kind that refused to die even when the neighborhood around it did.

Maya watched Paul Ellsworth park and enter.

As she circled the block, she wondered if she should just go home.

A parking spot near the rear of the nightclub opened up and she took it.

Inside the Pink Lady, the dining room was crowded and loud, the bar three deep with customers. But Maya's attention fixed on movement toward a velvet curtain near the back.

A large man stood in front of the split curtain wearing dark tinted glasses—completely unnecessary in the dim room.

She waited.

A guest approached, flashed something to the doorman, and the curtain parted briefly.

A flash of light spilled out, along with the hum of something private. Exclusive.

Then the curtain closed again.

A crash erupted from the kitchen—glass shattering, someone shouting in Spanish, angry voices rising.

The doorman turned toward the noise and pushed through the kitchen doors.

Maya moved.

She slipped behind the curtain and into the darkness.

Dimly lit stairs led downward into a cellar.

Voices drifted up.

One voice distinct and rhythmic.

"Twenty-five."

"Twenty-eight."

"Thirty-five."

She followed the sound.

Music thumped overhead, but down here cigarette smoke coiled through the air and the crowd was thick with shadows and wealth.

Velvet curtains draped the walls. Crystal glasses flashed under low lights.

Men in tailored suits and women in diamonds crowded around long tables stacked with crates.

At the center stood a woman—pearls draped at her throat, a fascinator pinned into carefully arranged hair, gloves gleaming under the lights.

She looked to be in her sixties. The makeup didn't soften her face; it sharpened the lines of age. The wig looked deliberate. Almost theatrical.

One by one, attendants unveiled the lots: handbags, watches, carved art objects.

Bids snapped through the room in clipped phrases, greed flashing in every nod.

Paul Ellsworth sat hunched nearby at a table, pen scratching numbers.

He looked smaller here.

Maya's throat tightened.

This was no punishment.

He was still in some kind of game.

She hadn't realized how close she'd drifted until a man turned.

"Don't think I've seen you before."

His eyes narrowed.

"Who brought you down here?"

Her blood ran cold.

He stepped toward her, suspicion hard in his gaze.

Maya bolted.

She darted between tables, the squeak of her sneakers swallowed by the music and startled murmurs of the crowd. She shoved through a swinging door into a narrow kitchen.

Pots rattled as she barreled past startled cooks.

Then she burst into the night air, lungs burning.

She didn't stop running until she reached her car.

Her hands trembled on the wheel.

But her eyes blazed.

She had seen enough to know Ellsworth wasn't just surviving.

He was part of something bigger.

Something rotten.

Maya's car tore out of the alley and disappeared into traffic.

The alley went quiet again.

From the mouth of the alley, a figure pressed herself into the shadow of a lamppost and watched the chaos spilling from the basement door.

A young woman—dark-haired, terrified—burst into the street running.

Within seconds she had jumped into her car.

Another woman stepped from the shadows near the alley mouth.

She raised the small camera she kept in her coat pocket.

Three quick frames:

The license plate of the fleeing car.

Crates being unloaded from a van.

The rear exit of the Pink Lady.

She checked the photos, pulse ticking fast.

This was it.

Enough to keep going.

That woman... who was she?

And what was she doing in there?

Clare Hinton's supervisor had told her not to take the lead seriously.

"We get tips like this every week," she had said. "That location's been checked before. Nothing there. Delete it."

But Clare wanted to see for herself.

The neon sign continued to flicker, its glow reflecting off the wet pavement.

Clare slipped her camera back into her coat and disappeared into the dark.

CHAPTER TEN

Turning Tide

* * *

TURNING TIDE — shift in direction of travel

* * *

Saturday morning sunlight streamed through the tall windows of the Oakland High School auditorium, warming rows of folding chairs that only an hour earlier had been filled with students, parents, and community leaders. Banners strung along the walls read Leadership in Action and Voices for Tomorrow, their edges stirring whenever the doors opened.

The morning had been alive with energy: youth practicing public speaking onstage, others debating environmental justice in tight circles, still more scribbling coalition-building ideas on butcher paper tacked to the walls. Fiona had manned a voter registration table near the entrance, her voice steady and persuasive as she spoke with parents and high school seniors about the power of the ballot. Across the room, Ben had guided a workshop on confident communication, urging students to claim their stories and speak with strength.

Now the crowd had thinned. The auditorium was quieter, filled only with the scrape of chairs being folded and stacked. Fiona and Ben lingered near the stage, watching the last clusters of students carry equipment into storage.

Fiona's gaze lingered on a group of teenagers balancing the podium between them.

"That turnout," she said softly. "Seeing them step up, register, speak out—it's why we do this. This is how you make real change."

Ben nodded, his eyes following the students.

"You're right. Standing here, it feels different. Not just words. Action."

He hesitated, then spoke with the weight of decision.

"I've been turning an idea over in my mind since Ellsworth's trial. Watching him walk free after stealing from this city made me furious. But after today, I'm more convinced than ever. I need to run for City Council."

Fiona turned toward him, her expression softening.

"Ben... you should. People trust you. They see what you stand for. And the timing matters. Strikes are looming—dockworkers, maybe BART, even AC Transit. If all those unions walk, the whole city will feel it. Voters are going to be desperate for someone who listens, someone who doesn't just posture. You could be that voice."

Ben gave a small, grim smile.

"Ellsworth poisoned the system from the inside. If I run, it won't be to play at politics. It'll be to fight from the inside, but for the people. Today proved it for me. We need leaders who remember who they're serving."

She reached out, resting her hand briefly on his arm.

"Then don't wait. If this is what you believe, you have to move now. The city needs people like you."

The last of the students pushed a cart of folded chairs toward the exit. The room emptied, leaving polished floors and bright walls echoing with the residue of the morning's voices. Ben stood still, the decision taking root in him like something that could no longer be undone.

That evening, Ben found himself in Wallace's workshop. The scent of motor oil and coffee hung in the air, grounding him in the familiar. Tools gleamed from hooks on the wall; the workbench bore scars from years of labor.

"I can't keep shouting from the sidelines," Ben said. "Ellsworth's debacle proved that. He siphoned off funds meant for neighborhoods and walked away with a fine. That kind of rot is exactly why I want to run for council."

Wallace studied him over the rim of his glasses, silent for a long moment.

"You know what you're stepping into?" Wallace finally asked. His voice was low, steady. "The port's on the edge. This campaign could be a powder keg."

Ben's jaw tightened, but his eyes didn't waver.

"That's exactly why it matters. People are fed up. Workers who've carried the city for decades, families who've been ignored, neighborhoods Ellsworth left in weeds and rubble. Someone has to stand up in the council chambers and say enough. Someone who won't fold the minute the pressure starts."

Wallace leaned back on his stool, arms folding across his chest.

"Then do it right. Speak plain. Speak true. Don't let them turn you into another suit."

Ben took a deep breath, the decision sharp and solid now.

"I won't."

CHAPTER ELEVEN

The Headwind

* * *

HEADWIND — resistance slowing progress.

* * *

The room smelled of sweat, coffee, and salty air. Folding chairs creaked under the weight of dockworkers who had seen too many contracts come and go.

At the front, the union representative read the statement flatly, though his voice carried the weight of finality.

"Negotiations have collapsed. Management walked away. As of midnight, the contract expires. We strike at dawn."

A rumble spread through the hall, fists slamming against tabletops. Thomas Forrester stood near the back, arms crossed, his jaw set like concrete. He'd expected this.

Another rep raised his voice over the noise.

"No crane turns. No truck rolls. We built this port with our backs, and we'll shut it down the same way until they come back to the table."

Thomas's voice cut through, clear and commanding.

"We do this right. No violence. No slip-ups. We hold the line together, or not at all."

A chorus of agreement answered him.

Tomorrow the port would go silent.

* * *

By morning, the gates of the Port of Oakland were ringed with men in jackets and hard hats, holding signs that read FAIR CONTRACTS NOW and NO CONTRACT, NO WORK.

Trucks idled in long rows, drivers leaning against bumpers, smoke curling from their cigarettes. The cranes loomed above, massive and still, their arms fixed against the sky.

Helicopters circled. News vans clustered near the gates, cameras trained on the picket lines.

The strike had begun.

On television, anchors seized on the split-screen story. One image showed the blue-and-gold jets of the Blue Angels slicing across the skies over San Francisco, Fleet Week banners snapping on the Embarcadero. The other showed Oakland—cranes frozen in silhouette, picket signs raised high, police standing at the edges.

Anchor One: "With Fleet Week still five days away, San Francisco prepares for Navy ships and air shows. But across the Bay, Oakland is making international headlines of its own. A full-scale port strike has shut down the West Coast's fourth busiest container hub. Economists warn the ripple effects could be felt nationwide within days."

Anchor Two: "And it is not stopping at the docks. Tonight, union leaders confirm that Bay Area Rapid Transit and Alameda County Transit workers are preparing to walk out in sympathy with the longshore workers. If those systems shut down, the impact will be staggering. More than 375,000 daily BART riders and another 200,000 AC Transit passengers will be left without service."

Anchor One: "That is nearly 600,000 commuters stranded every day, many of them dependent on those lines to cross the Bay Bridge or move through the East Bay."

Anchor Two: "Officials warn of gridlock, shortages, and cascading delays. The Bay Area may be heading into a perfect storm of celebration and paralysis."

The volume was low, but the café seemed to lean toward it, every table reacting in its own way.

"...my store's shipments are stuck on the water."

"...if they don't get parts moving, half the auto shops in Alameda shut down."

"...good for the workers. Somebody had to stand up."

At the back table, Rich, Maya, Ben, and Fiona sat with their mugs untouched. The news ticker crawled across the screen above them, and the tension in the room pressed down like another body at their table.

"This is it," Rich said, gesturing around. "Everyone is talking about it. Picket lines in Oakland, parades in San Francisco. Same Bay, different worlds."

Fiona leaned in, her voice urgent.

"But look around. People are awake. They're asking questions. They're connecting the dots. That's how change starts."

Ben swirled his tea, steam curling upward. His voice was quieter, steadier.

"Or how divisions deepen. Fleet Week is about unity, but Oakland is telling a different story. If Ellsworth were still in office, he would spin this strike into proof the city is ungovernable."

Maya shook her head.

"This isn't about optics. It's about survival. Dad says the men can't keep working without protections. They've drawn the line."

At a nearby table, two dockworkers argued heatedly with a young couple.

"You can't just stop everything. People rely on this port."

"And we rely on these jobs. No contract, no work. Simple as that."

The tension rippled through the café, sharp as the hiss of the espresso machine.

Ben set his mug down, the porcelain striking wood with finality. He looked at the three of them, his voice calm but edged with conviction.

"I've been quiet long enough. After Ellsworth, after everything we saw in court, after today's broadcast, there's no doubt in my mind. I've decided to run for City Council, District Five. I submitted my application today."

The table fell silent. Around them, conversations swelled and crashed like waves, the city itself arguing over its future.

At their table, the decision had been made.

* * *

The last truck to slip out of port bound for the warehouse caught the attention of police. The driver rolled through a red turn too fast, cutting off an SUV that had the right-of-way. A horn blared. The sound bled into the whoop of a cruiser's siren. Flashing lights filled his mirrors.

He pulled to the curb, knuckles gripping the wheel. Sweat slicked his palms. This was supposed to be routine, another quiet haul.

Two officers stepped out, flashlights slicing across the cab.

"License and registration."

He fumbled through the glove box, pulling out his license but coming up empty on the registration. The compartment gaped with crumpled papers, old napkins, nothing that looked official.

The officers traded a look.

"Step out of the vehicle."

He obeyed, heart hammering as they circled the truck. One yanked the rear latch. The doors groaned open, revealing crates stacked neatly inside, brands and logos glinting under the beam of a flashlight.

Electronics. Handbags. Watches.

The younger officer let out a low whistle.

"You want to tell us what you're hauling?"

His mouth went dry.

This was the moment he had been prepped for.

If you ever get stopped, you've got one name to give. Forrester. Say he trained you. Say he covered it. They'll believe that. They won't dig further.

The flashlight swung back to his face.

"Whose load is this?"

His voice cracked, desperation breaking through.

"Forrester. Thomas Forrester trained me. Said he'd cover it."

The officers jotted down the name without hesitation. A hand turned him toward the hood, cold cuffs locking around his wrists.

As they led him to the cruiser, Marty kept his eyes down, repeating the name in his head like a shield.

Forrester.

CHAPTER TWELVE

Manifests

* * *

Manifests — document listing a ship's cargo, passengers, or crew.

* * *

The next morning, the picket lines were already humming when two police cars eased up to the gates. The rumble of chants faltered as the cars rolled to a stop and the doors opened. Four officers stepped out—City of Oakland badges flashing on their belts, the kind that made a crowd tense even before a word was spoken.

Their eyes swept the line, passing faces hardened by years of labor until one of them called out, "Thomas Forrester?"

Two officers moved straight toward him.

Before he could answer, one of them took his arm and turned him around. Cold steel snapped around his wrists.

His picket sign fell to the ground.

The line erupted.

"Hey! What the hell—"

"That's Tom!"

Camera crews swung away from the picketers and toward the commotion as another officer stepped between the crowd and the arrest.

Only then did the first officer speak, voice flat and official.

"You are under arrest for theft from shipping containers at the Port of Oakland."

The words hit like a hammer. Murmurs surged through the crowd.

Forrester's jaw set. "You've got the wrong man."

The officers formed a semicircle, wary hands near their belts. Thomas raised his chin, signaling to the men.

"Easy," he said, his voice steady, carrying across the noise. "Don't give them a reason."

The crowd parted as the officers took his arm and walked him toward the cruiser.

"You have the right to remain silent. Anything you say can and will be used..." an officer recited as they marched Thomas away from the crowd.

Cameras clicked. Someone started filming on a phone.

By the time the doors shut and the cars rolled away, the strike had a new wound—and everyone on the line knew the story would hit the news before noon.

* * *

Maya's phone buzzed where it lay among open notebooks and a half-eaten sandwich. She had been buried in notes, piecing through timelines and union statements. The screen flashed: **Mom**.

She answered. "Hey, Mom—"

"Maya." Doris's voice trembled. "They just picked up your father. At the gates. They said his name was tied to stolen merchandise from containers at the port."

Maya froze, pen still in her hand. "What? That's impossible."

"They're saying he trained the driver who got caught. Everyone saw him taken from the line."

Maya pushed back from the table, her chair scraping hard against the floor.

"No. No, he—he told me he thought something shady was going on. They're turning it on him?"

"They didn't give him a choice," Doris said, her breath catching. "Your grandfather's furious. We've called a lawyer. They say he won't spend the night in jail, but it's all over the news already—he's being accused of grand theft and conspiracy."

The words blurred.

Maya grabbed the remote and started flipping through channels until the strike coverage appeared.

"Mom, I'm coming right now."

"Stay put," Doris said quickly. "There's nothing you can do yet."

The call ended, but the silence it left roared in her ears.

She turned, pulse hammering, and found Rich watching her as the footage filled the screen.

"What's happening?" he asked, following her gaze.

"They arrested my dad," she said, her voice breaking. "At the line. Said he was tied to stolen cargo."

Rich blinked, stunned. "What? How—?"

"I don't know." She started pacing. "But it's not random. He told me last week he thought something was off—trucks coming and going late at night. He reported it. Now they're pinning it on him."

Rich ran a hand through his hair. "That's insane. Why would they—"

She stopped pacing and met his eyes.

"Because someone's making money off it. And I think I've already seen who."

He frowned. "What do you mean?"

Maya hesitated, then the words tumbled out.

"After the verdict, I followed Paul Ellsworth. He went to this place in Jack London Square, a club called the Pink Lady. It wasn't just a club, Rich. It was an auction. Crates stacked against the walls, people bidding on watches, handbags—stolen goods, I think. And Ellsworth was there, taking notes, like he was part of it."

Rich's expression went rigid. "You did what? You followed Ellsworth? Alone?"

"It's not about me," she snapped. "I'm fine."

He stepped closer, his voice low but sharp. "Maya, that man is dangerous. You could have been—"

"This isn't about me!" she shot back. "It's about my dad."

Rich stared at her, torn between anger and fear.

"You can't just go chasing after—"

"I'm not chasing," she cut in. "If the system protects men like Ellsworth, then someone has to see what they're hiding."

Her phone buzzed again—a text from her mother.

He's on his way home. Released. But they've seized his pass. He can't go back to the yard.

Maya looked up, eyes bright with fury.

"They've already taken his name. I'm not letting them take his truth too."

* * *

By morning the rumor had a pulse. A respected trainer, a thirty-year veteran of the docks, suddenly painted as the man behind a load of stolen cargo. In the union hall, men muttered in disbelief.

"Forrester? No way. He's trained half of us."

But the name was written down in a police report, and once spoken aloud, it spread like oil on water.

At the Forrester house that evening, Captain Harper paced the living room, fists clasped behind his back.

"Thirty years breaking your back for that port, and they humiliate you like a criminal? If they think they can smear your name to cover their incompetence, they're going to regret it."

Thomas sat stiff in his chair, released but not cleared. His silence was heavier than his anger—the look of a man betrayed by the job he'd given his life to.

Doris hovered close, steady but shaken.

"The lawyer says we'll fight it. But in the meantime..."

She didn't finish.

CHAPTER THIRTEEN

Broken Compass

* * *

BROKEN COMPASS — instrument unable to find true north.

* * *

Fiona moved like a conductor at the center of it all. She had commandeered the back of the café into a campaign hub, walls plastered with maps and voter lists, a long table crowded with phones, buttons, and stacks of registration cards.

"Phone bank starts at five," she reminded the volunteers, sliding clipboards into eager hands. "Every new voter you register is a voice they can't ignore."

Ben walked in, jacket slung over his arm, tie loosened after another long day of canvassing. He looked tired, but his eyes burned with purpose.

"How'd we do?"

Fiona grinned. "Seventy-five calls tonight. Twenty-two new registrations. Not bad for a Tuesday."

Uncle Wallace leaned against the counter, arms folded but his face open with pride.

"You're hitting the right notes, Benny. People don't just want to hear you; they need to feel your heart. That matters."

The campaign was getting started and they didn't have long before election day. Ben shook hands outside the library, planned to walk picket lines with dockworkers, knock on doors in Fruitvale and West Oakland. At each stop his message would be steady, unpolished, but real.

"I'm not a politician," he told one cluster of voters on a corner lot. "I worked in city planning. I've seen the records, the contracts, the promises that never reached our neighborhoods. I know how much was stolen, and I know how much more we can build if we start telling the truth again. That's why I'm running. Because Oakland deserves better."

People nodded. Some shook his hand, others just took a button or a flyer, but the support was visible. Signs went up. Chatter grew. His name carried.

A local radio station invited him on air. The host's questions were pointed.

"You're young. You don't have money behind you. How do you expect to compete against entrenched power?"

Ben's answer was simple.

"With people. With every voter who's tired of seeing the same suits make the same excuses. This isn't about me, it's about us. It's about making sure our city belongs to its people again."

Fiona listened from the campaign office, her smile widening as the phone lit up with callers asking where they could get signs, how they could help.

A rally was held on the steps of the old courthouse, the crowd swelling with striking workers, families, students, and neighbors carrying homemade signs. Fiona made sure the microphones worked, that volunteers passed out flyers, that campaign buttons were clipped to jackets.

Ben stood near the podium, shaking hands, listening as people told him their stories, rent hikes, jobs lost, promises broken. His nerves hummed, but the fire in him burned steady.

At the edge of the crowd, his mother threaded her way forward with Grandy at her side, Wallace close behind. She reached him just before he stepped up to the microphone.

"Hold still," she said softly, fussing with the knot of his tie, smoothing it against his shirtfront. Her eyes shone, her voice catching. "Your father would be so proud. We all are."

Grandy tapped her cane once against the stone steps, nodding.

"You've got the voice for this, Ben. Strong. Don't let them rattle you."

Wallace, gruff but warm, clasped his nephew's shoulder.

"Speak plain. Speak true. That's what'll carry you."

Rich slid in at the last second, flashing a grin and snapping a photo.

"And don't forget to smile. You're not auditioning for a funeral, man—you're trying to get votes."

Ben chuckled, the tension in his chest easing just enough. He looked at the four of them, his family, his anchor, his brother-in-arms, and then at the sea of faces waiting for him to speak.

"I won't let you down," he said quietly.

Then he stepped up to the podium, ready to speak to the city.

Ben gripped the sides of the podium, scanning the crowd. Striking workers in union jackets. Parents holding kids on their shoulders. Students waving homemade signs. Neighbors who had lived the same broken promises he had.

"Good evening, Oakland," he began, his voice steady but unpolished. "You know me. I'm not a politician. I don't have lobbyists or a team polishing my every word. What I have is this."

He held up a worn notebook, the same one he carried from house to house.

"Your stories. What you've told me as I've walked these streets, as I've listened outside grocery stores, libraries, union halls. You've told me what's not working. And I'm here because I believe we can fix it."

Murmurs of agreement rippled through the crowd.

"I worked in city planning. I saw how the records looked neat on paper while neighborhoods crumbled. I watched funds disappear into contracts that never brought results. And I know how it feels to lose trust in the very people who swore they represented you. That's why I'm running. Because I'm done waiting for someone else to fix it."

He paused, his eyes catching the faces in the front row—his mother, Grandy, Wallace, Rich, Fiona. The people who meant the most in his life.

"This city deserves honesty. It deserves accountability. And it deserves leaders who remember where they came from. I don't want to be another suit at a podium. I want to be your voice inside those chambers. And I promise you this—"

He leaned forward, his voice carrying, strong and certain. "If you give me that chance, I will not let this city down."

A harsh voice cut across the cheer that followed.

"He's lying to you!"

Ben saw him then.

Paul Ellsworth.

The same man who had walked out of court smiling.

Heads turned. Paul Ellsworth shoved forward from the edge of the crowd, jacket crooked, hair damp with sweat.

"Ask him what he's ever built!"

"Ask him what he's ever run except his mouth!"

"He's a clerk with a grudge, not a leader!"

Boos rose from the crowd, drowning him out, along with murmurs of "Is that Paul Ellsworth?"

"Didn't he just—"

But Paul kept shouting.

"He's lying to you! Every word he says. He lies!"

Ben steadied himself at the podium, refusing to look away.

"Mr. Ellsworth once told me the city belonged to men like him. The powerful. The connected." He spread a hand toward the crowd. "But look around you. Tonight, the city answers him for me."

The chants swelled, rolling like thunder across the steps.

"Coo-per! Coo-per!"

Security edged Paul back, his last words cracking thin against the roar.

As the commotion spread and security pressed in around Paul, a woman near the edge of the crowd didn't move. She hadn't raised a sign or joined the chant, hadn't flinched when his voice rose or softened when it cracked.

While others turned toward the stage or craned to see what the commotion meant, her attention stayed fixed on Ellsworth—on the way his shoulders squared when he realized he'd been noticed, on how quickly indignation settled into a familiar rhythm.

When he was finally ushered away and the noise smoothed back into applause, she wrote something in a small notebook, tore out the page, and folded it once.

She didn't stay for the closing remarks.

By the time Ben stepped back to the microphone and the crowd leaned in again, she was already gone.

Fiona beamed from the sidelines, Rich pumped a fist in the air, and Ben stepped back, humbled but certain: the campaign was real, and the people were with him.

CHAPTER FOURTEEN

The Waterline

* * *

WATERLINE — point at which a hull meets the water

* * *

Clare heard it while pouring coffee, the local anchor's voice cutting through the hum of her refrigerator.

"—Thomas Forrester, a thirty-year veteran of the Port of Oakland, was taken into custody in connection with the theft of merchandise from shipping containers. Police allege—"

She froze, mug halfway to her lips.

Forrester.

The name snapped into place like a puzzle piece. She set the mug down, grabbed her notebook from the table, and flipped through the pages until she found it—the same surname she had scrawled in the margin after the port incident.

Forrester.

Her pulse quickened.

So, she hadn't imagined it.

She spread the documents across the table, aligning them by date, her movements crisp and precise. The foreman, the one who'd told her accidents happen, was being named as the culprit.

Her supervisor's voice echoed in memory: *You're paid to verify paperwork. That's all.*

Clare closed the notebook.

"Not anymore," she murmured.

* * *

Maya's apartment looked like a storm had passed through. Papers littered the table, notebooks lay open at odd angles, her laptop glowing with too many tabs to count. The takeout Rich had brought hours earlier sat untouched, its foil lids collapsing inward.

Her father's arrest looped in her mind like a broken reel: Thomas Forrester pulled from the picket line, men shouting his name, cameras flashing, his jaw locked in silence as they led him away.

Thirty years of work buried under one false accusation.

Maya's pen tapped furiously against the page.

"They think they can pin this on him. Like he'd risk everything—his name, his crew? No. Somebody's hiding something. Burying it. But not everything can vanish. It can't."

Rich leaned against the counter, arms folded loosely, watching her pace. He wanted to reach for her, but didn't. Not yet.

"May, you've been at this for hours. Talk to me. What are you really chasing here?"

She stopped, breath quick, eyes sharp.

"Proof. Something that shows Dad had nothing to do with this."

Rich tilted his head. "You don't think his lawyer's already pulling every thread?"

"I won't just sit around and wait," she snapped, her voice rising. "This is his life, Rich. His reputation. Everything he stands for."

Her hand raked through her hair. She kept pacing, quick and restless.

"So what do you expect me to do? Sit here while they drag his name through the mud?"

"You don't sit," Rich said carefully. "You plan. That's what you're good at. You see patterns where other people skim past. No one I know is as detailed as you are, May. Use that. Tomorrow, start with the people you trust most—talk to your mom again, maybe Wallace."

Maya sank into her chair, notebook open in front of her. Her hands trembled slightly as she pressed the pen to the page.

"I can't keep doing nothing while this city chews up my dad. I need to know what's real."

Rich finally stepped closer, resting a hand on the back of her chair.

"And you will. But not tonight. Don't burn yourself out before you've even begun. You've got me, Ben, and Fiona too. You don't have to do this alone."

Her eyes softened, though the fire in them didn't dim.

"Tomorrow," she said quietly. "I start tomorrow."

Rich nodded, a flicker of relief crossing his face. "Tomorrow."

But as Maya bent over her notes again, scribbling connections with manic precision, Rich couldn't shake the coil of worry tightening in his chest.

CHAPTER FIFTEEN

Slip Number Seven

* * *

SLIP — a designated berth for docking a vessel.

* * *

Sunlight spilled through the blinds and painted the apartment in tidy bands of gold.

Clare poured food into the fish tank, watching the single betta, Marlowe, rise to the surface. Its scales flared iridescent in the light—blue, then green, then blue again—before the fish sank back into the filtered murk.

The rest of the apartment was as precise as the tank: one bookshelf alphabetized by author, a stack of inspection files on the desk, a kettle left warming on the stove. The kind of order that disguised solitude.

She stirred a spoonful of sugar into her coffee and replayed the photos she'd taken the night before: the alley, the crates, the woman running. Each image felt like a secret only she possessed.

At noon the doorbell buzzed. Clare checked the peephole and smiled.

"Right on time," she called, unlocking the deadbolt.

The members of her book club trickled in, four women from her building, arms full of pastries and paperbacks. They had met every other weekend for years, reading thrillers and domestic mysteries that always promised that one smart woman could untangle the lies of the world.

"This month's choice," Lisa said, fanning the cover of *Gone Girl*, "reminded me of you, Clare. All that forensic detail."

Clare laughed lightly. "Hopefully with fewer dead husbands."

They settled around the coffee table, crumbs gathering on napkins as they debated endings and motives. When conversation drifted, as it always did, to neighborhood gossip and office grievances, Lisa tilted her head.

"You've been quiet. Working on something interesting?"

Clare hesitated, savoring the attention.

"Can't say much. It's... ongoing."

That was all it took.

"Another smuggling case?"

"Tell us you're chasing bad guys again!"

She feigned reluctance. "Really, I shouldn't. It's off the record."

They pressed harder, delighted by the hint of danger. The air filled with their laughter and the clink of coffee spoons. Finally, Clare sighed, smiling as if defeated.

"All right—but this stays between us."

She leaned forward, lowering her voice.

"You remember those ivory seizures in the papers last spring? Everyone said the trail went cold. Well, it didn't. I got a tip and last night I did a little surveillance."

The women gasped in unison. Lisa's eyes were wide.

"You mean like a stakeout?"

"Not officially," Clare admitted, pleased by their shock. "There was a woman on the scene—young, dark hair, ran when the lights hit her. I think she's connected."

"Clare-Bear, that's wild," someone breathed. "You have to tell us what happens next!"

"I will," she promised, basking in their excitement.

For the first time in months, she felt visible. Important. The woman who always followed rules now carried a story too thrilling to keep.

When her friends left an hour later, she walked them to the door, accepting their hugs and mock salutes.

Be careful, Agent Hinton!

When the apartment fell silent again, Clare fed the fish a second time, watching as it flicked its tail and vanished into the plants. She smiled faintly, already planning her next steps—pull the port manifests again, trace vehicle registrations near Jack London Square, find out who the dark-haired woman was. By then, the name Forrester was already needling at her.

* * *

Doris sent a text to her daughter, **Call me when you're free.** Maya was happy to have a distraction. Her eyes were tired from the constant screen time and research she was doing on her dad's case.

Rising from her seat at the island in her kitchen, she poured herself a fresh cup of coffee and dialed her mom.

"Hi, Mom." Maya added cream and sugar to her coffee and stirred, waiting for the reassurance she assumed was coming.

"May, listen, I know you're trying to do everything you can to help your father," she began. Here it comes, Maya thought. A reminder not to worry.

"—and I was just thinking," Doris continued, her voice brisk but warm. "We used to keep redundancies at Naval Supply. Nothing ever really disappeared. If something got changed on the daily report, the originals were still somewhere in the system."

Maya straightened. She grabbed her pencil, pausing over her notebook.

"So, if someone altered the front-end logs..." She turned back to the screen. "They couldn't erase the underlying record."

"That was my understanding."

"Backups," Maya said softly and she felt the first spark of hope she'd had since her father's arrest.

"Thanks, Mom. If that's true, I can find evidence to prove Dad is innocent. I'll call you later tonight."

She hung up and turned to her laptop. Data columns glowed in pale blue light—arrival times, cargo IDs, clerk signatures.

After hours of staring, a pattern emerged: repeating timestamps, duplicated IDs, gaps where containers should have been.

Her pulse quickened.

Someone had erased the truth, but not everywhere.

* * *

By early afternoon, she was at the Port Authority.

The waiting room smelled of stale coffee and paper. Faded posters of cranes and cargo ships lined the walls. A man in a rumpled suit flipped through her printouts without interest.

"These are anomalies, sure," he said. "But nothing here proves wrongdoing."

"The data is corrupted," Maya said, leaning forward. "Either shipments are lost or they're stolen. Check the originals against the reports. You'll see."

He sighed. "Ms. Forrester, your father has just been released on suspicion of theft. You're not a port employee. You have no standing here."

Maya's eyes blazed.

"The evidence is right in front of you. At least look."

"You've made your concerns known."

He slid the papers back across the desk.

"Next."

Outside, the Bay wind caught her hair and stung her eyes. She gripped her notebook, anger and helplessness coiling together. They weren't going to listen. She'd have to make them.

* * *

That afternoon, Maya sat across from her dad's lawyer in an office off Webster Street in Alameda. The desk was weighed down with files. Today's newspaper headlines were clearly visible from the East Bay Times and Maya could read the headline even though to her the letters were upside down and reversed: CRANES STILL SILENT. COMMUTERS STRANDED. NEGOTIATIONS COLLAPSE.

Thomas's voice crackled over the speakerphone, gravel and fatigue mixed together. "They've tied my name to this theft. My record was clean. Never so much as a violation."

The attorney glanced down at another file. "One more thing. Marty Butler made bail three nights ago."

Maya froze. "Then he can help clear my dad's name."

"Only if we can find him," the attorney said. "So far, no luck."

Maya spread her printouts across the desk, refusing to be still.

"We know shipments are disappearing. The Port Authority's blocking us, saying access is restricted. But those manifests exist. If we can get them, we've got proof there's something bigger going on out there and my father is not involved."

The attorney tapped his pen, thinking.

"Management doesn't want lawsuits, not with the strike choking them. If they think I'll go public with how they're stonewalling, they'll fold."

Within hours, the pressure worked. Maya was granted temporary access to the port's database through a secure portal.

Thomas's attorney suggested she use an empty office in the law firm's Alameda building.

"I'll stay and finish up," she told him when he started packing his briefcase. "Just a few hours."

He nodded. "Don't stay too late. Security is light after six."

* * *

Across the street, Clare Hinton watched Maya enter the office building from her car, notebook open on the steering wheel.

She had already run the license plate. Registered owner: Maya Forrester. The name had stopped her cold—Forrester.

Pink Lady. Maya Forrester. Port of Oakland. Thomas Forrester. It could be a coincidence. Clare no longer believed that.

Her phone buzzed on the seat beside her again.

Supervisor – FWS HQ

She ignored it.

Another buzz.

Call me. Field reports due.

Clare flipped the phone face-down. The screen dimmed, leaving her reflection faint and accusing in the glass. She wasn't about to file reports about confiscated pelts when an entire smuggling ring was unfolding under her nose.

Marlowe swam lazy circles in his travel cup wedged into the cup holder, the water shimmering in the weak afternoon light.

"This is more important," she muttered, watching Maya cross the street, shoulders tense. "You'll see."

She noted the time—2:43 p.m.

* * *

The office was silent except for the hum of her laptop and the wind off the estuary rattling the windows.

By 8pm, Maya had confirmation: shipments reappearing under new IDs, time-stamped after hours, signatures falsified.

The proof she'd been chasing.

Her exhaustion melted into grim satisfaction. She saved her files, double-checked the drive, and rubbed her eyes.

When she stepped into the hallway, the building felt hollow. She hadn't realized until now how alone she really was in the office. Her movements echoed off the concrete surroundings.

The parking garage below was abandoned, fluorescent lights flickering over the lone car she had left behind. The sound of her own footfall set her teeth on edge. Each echo seemed to come back a second later, slightly off time, like someone walking just behind her.

Heartbeat thudding, she fumbled for her keys and ducked into her car, locking the doors before she started the engine.

She exhaled once. Twice.

Get a grip, May.

The exit ramp spiraled up into the empty street, and she turned back toward Oakland.

* * *

Clare was still there.

She had been there all day, surviving on corner store coffee and adrenaline. "I'm working," she muttered. "Just not for them." The Fish and Wildlife phone had finally buzzed itself into silence around 6pm.

Through the windshield, she saw movement: the woman from the auction leaving the building's parking structure alone. Clare straightened. The streetlight caught the curve of Maya's face as she pulled her car onto the street.

"Got you," Clare whispered.

She started her own car, headlights off until Maya cleared the intersection. Marlowe's travel cup sloshed water in the cupholder as she made the turn.

"Sorry, partner," she said to the fish. "Occupational hazard."

The first few blocks were easy—steady distance, easy tail. But when Maya's car slowed at a red light, Clare, distracted by the spilled water, nearly clipped the curb.

She swore under her breath.

Maya noticed the headlights in her mirror as the car behind her skidded noticeably out of the lane.

The light turned green.

She turned left.

The car followed.

She sped up.

So did the car behind her.

By the time the entrance to the Posey Tube opened ahead, Maya's nerves had dissolved into pure instinct. She pressed the accelerator. The tunnel swallowed her in a rush of light and noise.

Behind her, Clare followed, adrenaline drowning out reason. The tunnel narrowed to one open lane; orange cones scattered along the divider. Marlowe's cup tipped in the holder, water sloshing up the sides.

"Damn it—"

Clare jerked the wheel to avoid a cone, clipping another that flipped under her tires. The sound echoed like a gunshot. She floored the gas to keep pace, eyes fixed on the red taillights ahead.

Maya's hands clenched on the wheel. The tunnel curved, walls flashing close. Her speedometer hit sixty.

Don't panic. Don't brake.

The exit loomed ahead, the light changing from green to yellow. She shot through, her tires lifting slightly as she hit the rise and flew through the intersection just as the signal turned red behind her.

When she glanced in the rearview mirror, the other car was gone—lost somewhere in the long orange throat of the tunnel.

Maya slowed only when she reached the first familiar street in Oakland. She pulled to the curb, chest heaving, the silence in her car almost unreal.

She looked in the mirror once more. Empty road.

CHAPTER SIXTEEN

The Harbor Line

* * *

HARBOR LINE — legal boundary of a port's jurisdiction.

* * *

The chase still lived under her skin. Even after the long drive home and Rich's whispered reassurances that she was safe, Maya couldn't stop replaying the image of headlights in her rearview mirror—too close, too fast.

When she finally drifted into sleep, her mind didn't rest.

She dreamt she was back at the harbor that night.

Thomas and Maya drove down to Middle Harbor, slipping through a gap in the fence and keeping to the shadows.

From the edge of the park, the port stretched out before them, cranes lit like skeletons against the sky.

On the access road, box trucks idled at the gate. Men moved under dim floodlights, crates shifting hand to hand with practiced speed.

Thomas squinted. "This is it. Shipments peeled off before they ever hit the books."

Maya crouched low, scribbling plate numbers into her notebook.

"If we trace these, we can prove it."

Floodlights snapped toward them—blinding white.

"Hey!"

Three men in port-security jackets stormed across the lot.

Before Maya could run, rough hands clamped down, wrenching the notebook from her grip. Thomas lunged, but a blow to his ribs sent him reeling against the side of a truck.

The rear doors groaned open.

"Get inside."

They were shoved hard, tumbling into the dark interior. The latch slammed.

Blackness. Motion. Metal. Heat.

The floor pitched beneath her, every turn throwing her sideways.

The truck jolted forward, hurling them across the metal floor. Zip-ties bit into their wrists, arms taut behind their backs. Every turn slammed Thomas into steel.

Maya twisted onto her stomach, chin grinding against the ridges. With a desperate stretch she freed her phone, pinning it beneath her jaw.

She flailed until she found the button for the last number called and pushed it with the tip of her nose.

It rang.

A click.

Rich's voice. "May?"

"Help!" Her voice came ragged, muffled. "Kidnapped—box truck—hurry—"

The line went dead.

"Damn it!" She bit her lip, choking back panic.

The phone buzzed again, Rich calling back.

Maya lunged, catching it before it slid away.

"Where are you?" Rich shouted.

Thomas pressed his face to the seam of the door.

"Shell station—big neon sign! Seventh Street—warehouses—red graffiti!"

Maya shouted into the phone, her voice shaking.

A new sound cut through—the rising wail of a train. The truck ground to a halt.

"We've stopped," she gasped. "At the tracks!"

Her gaze caught her notebook wedged in a corner. She kicked it toward Thomas. He trapped it under one boot.

Maya scrambled, a pen clenched between her teeth, scrawling awkward letters across the page:

HELP

She ripped the sheet free with her teeth, and together they shoved it through the crack beneath the door.

Outside, two motorcyclists waiting at the crossing glanced down as the paper skittered past. Helmeted heads turned. One bent, lifting it to the glow of a headlamp.

HELP

They didn't hesitate.

One sprang up and unlatched the truck's rear doors.

Light flooded in—pure, blinding—

* * *

Maya woke hard, tangled in sweat-soaked sheets, the morning light pressing around her. Her pulse refused to slow. She sat up, heart hammering, the sunlight in her room nothing like the darkness of the truck's void.

From the kitchen she could hear the low murmur of voices—Rich and her father, talking.

She pulled on her robe, stepped into the light, and said, "I think I found something."

The conference room at the Oakland Police Department smelled faintly of old carpet and older coffee. A whiteboard covered one wall, scrawled with half-erased notes from some unrelated case.

Two detectives sat across from Maya, Thomas, and his attorney—veterans with the look of men who had seen every excuse.

Detective Alvarez flipped open his notebook.

The attorney rested a hand lightly on the table. "We're here to present evidence, not speculation."

"We're listening," Alvarez said. His tone suggested otherwise.

Maya set her laptop on the table and angled the screen toward them.

"These are pulled directly from the Port Authority portal. I cross-referenced them against vessel records going back months."

Detective Chen, younger, leaned forward.

"Show us."

Maya tapped through the files, voice steady despite the thrum of nerves beneath it.

"Ports run on codes," she said quietly. "Manifests. Container IDs. Dock assignments. The ship's manifest logs thirty-seven containers unloaded. The port record shows thirty-six. That's one missing."

She clicked to the next file.

"Now here—same discrepancy, same clerk signature. And again the following month. It's deliberate. Shipments are logged in on one system and erased in the other. Change the code and the whole harbor lies."

Thomas leaned in, his voice gravelly but sure.

"I've worked those yards thirty years. Records don't just vanish. There are three layers—ship, dock, yard. If they don't match, you flag it. Unless someone wants it buried."

Alvarez and Chen exchanged a look. The skepticism in their posture began to ease.

"I didn't find this by accident," Maya said. "Someone is manipulating the system."

Chen tapped his pen against the table.

"If this holds, it's enough to put pressure on somebody we already have our eye on."

Part II

September - Elsewhere

CHAPTER SEVENTEEN

Dry Dock

* * *

DRY DOCK — a vessel is placed out of water for inspection or repair.

* * *

September

Flashbulbs flared as Paul Ellsworth stepped down the courthouse stairs. He adjusted his cufflinks, lifted his chin, and smiled for the cameras as though restitution and community service were a promotion. Inside, his stomach twisted with rage.

A black limousine eased from the curb. The rear door swung open.

Mallory Thornton waited inside. Her belted coat framed her sharply; gloves lay folded in her lap. The wide-brimmed hat shadowed her face, but her green eyes were clear, unblinking, and fixed on his.

"Get in, Paul," she said.

The door shut behind him, sealing out the crowd.

Paul sank into the seat, breath still tight from the cameras. "They should have never brought charges," he said. "This never should have touched a courtroom."

For a moment, the car hummed in silence.

"You're alive, Paul," Mallory said evenly. "A trial like that could have left you in a cell for much longer. Instead, you are free. Humbled, yes. But alive. And with another chance."

Paul let out a bitter laugh. "Free? I am a joke. The papers crucified me. Everything I built—"

"Everything you borrowed," she corrected.

The limousine slid into late-afternoon traffic, its tinted glass muting the last of the camera flashes. Ellsworth loosened his tie, though the knot seemed to tighten all the same. Mallory sat opposite him, her presence filling the cabin like a queen on a throne no one dared question.

The driver merged onto the 580 freeway eastbound, the city blurring past in streaks of concrete and glass. Billboards Paul had once approved rose along the corridor, advertising condominium towers, banks, sleek tech startups. He remembered ribbon cuttings, handshakes, speeches about renewal. Now the buildings looked indifferent, monuments to someone else's ambition.

Empty lots he had promised to "activate" were still bare, choked with weeds and rusted fencing. Not for the first time, he wondered whether his efforts had left any mark at all, or whether the city had simply shrugged him off and kept moving.

The limo turned off the freeway and wound through quiet, manicured streets toward the hills. Houses grew larger as they climbed, estates hidden behind clipped hedges and wrought-iron gates. He felt the throbbing at his temple begin to ease as home came into view. His own gates swung open at the car's approach, groaning on hinges he did not remember sounding so tired.

He stepped onto the driveway and froze.

The house rose before him, familiar but diminished, as if the year away had leached its grandeur.

Inside, the air was stale. The echo of his footsteps told him what his eyes had not yet fully processed: the place was hollow. Paintings had been stripped from the walls, leaving pale rectangles like scars. Sculptures were gone from their pedestals.

The grand Steinway that had anchored the foyer was gone. The room was cavernous. Sound itself seemed to have abandoned it.

Paul stood in the gutted silence and felt smaller than he ever had.

His voice cracked when he turned to face her. "What have you done?"

Mallory's tone was calm, almost sympathetic. "Sold what had value. Lawyers do not work for free. And since you were deemed a flight risk, keeping you safe at Santa Rita came at a price. None of it was cheap."

His fists clenched. "My collection was mine."

"Your freedom is yours," she said. "That is the only thing that matters now."

She let the silence hang until his breathing steadied.

Then: "If you want it back—your power, your money—you'll work for it. On my terms."

Paul shut his eyes.

He was back in their mother's kitchen, Mallory's hand heavy on his shoulder, her voice sharp as she ordered him to take the blame for a vase she had smashed. Big sister, always in charge. And here she was again.

He opened his eyes, voice low. "And if I don't?"

Mallory smiled, small and sharp. "Then you will lose what little you have left."

She turned and walked toward the door, heels striking the tile in measured echoes. The silence she left behind was heavier than her presence.

When the taillights of the limo vanished down the driveway, Paul moved through the rooms that had once held the evidence of his wealth. The house was hollow now. Only his footsteps slapped against the bare floors. The sound was wrong, as though he were trespassing in his own life.

CHAPTER EIGHTEEN

The Brig

* * *

BRIG — a detention compartment aboard a vessel.

* * *

That first night, the fluorescent lights never dimmed. Their buzzing burrowed into his skull. The mattress on the cot was so thin he felt every weld in the frame beneath him.

The guards never called him Mr. Ellsworth. They called him by his PFN—Personal File Number—427165. The laughter that followed was worse than the insult.

He shook his head, trying to clear the memory, and reached for the bourbon decanter that was no longer there. Only a pale ring remained on the wood. His hand trembled as he set it flat, fingers splayed, as if he could anchor himself before drifting away again.

But the floor shifted, and he was back in the cell.

Inmates circled him in the cafeteria. One of them was wiry and tattooed, his eyes quick and mean. He leaned close enough for Ellsworth to smell stale coffee on his breath.

"My momma's house was all we had left, and your developer friends tore it down for a strip mall."

Ellsworth swallowed.

The man's hand shot out and gripped his collar.

"All my people are gone because they couldn't afford to stay. That's on you."

The grip released with a shove, sending him stumbling back against the wall. The words landed heavier than iron.

Lights out. The bolt slid. Metal against metal.

He flinched every night. That sound dragged him back decades, to his mother's kitchen and Mallory's shadow, telling him which lies to tell, which blame to take. Locked cupboards. Locked silences.

In the dark cell, he pressed his palms to his ears. Too old to cry, too frightened not to.

Now, in the gutted estate, the silence pressed just as hard. He whispered aloud, only to hear another voice answer:

"Maybe they were right."

The words did not echo. They simply hung there, small and raw, in a house that felt more like a cage.

By morning, the fear had hardened into something else: humiliation, sharp as glass, waiting in every reflection.

CHAPTER NINETEEN

The Floodgate

* * *

FLOODGATE — a gate controlling the flow of water.

* * *

The sedan rolled through the gates of a warehouse facility in West Oakland, past corrugated steel walls scribbled with faded graffiti. Inside, fluorescent lights buzzed overhead. Forklifts thrummed, horns beeped, and crews pried open truck doors, the sound of steel echoing like gunfire.

Mallory walked with her gloved hands clasped behind her back. Paul followed, slower, his eyes catching details—the cracked crates, the grease-slick floor, the way the men kept their heads down.

Santa Rita had taught him that details meant survival.

Watch everything.

"This is the pipeline, Paul," Mallory said. "The buyers arrive later."

A clerk at a folding table typed furiously, lines of code tearing through container IDs in the Port Authority system. Mallory gestured with a tilt of her chin.

"That's the ledger. The digital erasure. By morning, the manifests correct themselves. Without him, these crates would glow like flares."

Paul peered into a case of jeweled watches. Once, he would have admired them purely for their worth. Now he caught himself wondering why.

He shut the thought down before it reached his face.

"And then what?" he said. "We stack them in your warehouse forever?"

Her lips twitched, almost a smile. "No. They go to auction. Where do you think the contents of your estate ended up?"

The jab landed harder than he let on. His gaze lingered on the watches again, thinner now, almost brittle.

Mallory led him into a curtained side room. A makeshift stage stood ready: velvet ropes, folding chairs, a simple wooden lectern. Workers moved through with crates, unpacking select items—handbags, timepieces, a small statue draped in cloth.

"Every month, a different location," Mallory said. "Sometimes here. Sometimes a shuttered hotel ballroom. Sometimes a private residence. Never the same place twice. Clients are invited personally and thoroughly vetted. Wealthy enough to buy silence. Greedy enough not to ask questions."

Paul nodded as though the detail meant little, but he locked onto it immediately.

"And what guarantees they won't talk?"

Mallory's eyes flicked toward him, steady. "Fear. Exclusivity. These people live on the illusion that they're untouchable. They won't destroy their own playground."

He folded his arms, jaw tightening. "And if the bids don't come in high enough?"

"Then you push them higher," Mallory said. "That's your role. Read the room. Nudge egos. Make sure the final number leaves everyone satisfied. Everyone except the loser."

She let that settle before continuing.

"The money moves offshore. Clean, hidden, untraceable. Everyone gets paid—dockworkers, transport, inventory, security. The machine keeps moving."

Paul let the words hang.

He noticed how the workers glanced at him when they thought he wasn't looking—some with suspicion, others with quiet contempt.

He wasn't the king here.

Not yet.

"So," he said lightly, "I'm the auctioneer's assistant?"

"You're the steward," she corrected. "I'm giving you a seat at the table. Don't confuse that with the head of it."

The weight of her words settled into him. For a flicker, he was young again—Mallory's voice directing him, shaping him, deciding what he would say and what he would carry.

His smirk returned, thinner now. "Fine. But I expect more than scraps."

Mallory's smile didn't reach her eyes. "Earn it first."

* * *

Two days later, Paul sat in a dull government office, the stench of disinfectant thick in the air. A parole officer in a short-sleeved shirt thumbed through his file without looking up.

"Two hundred hours of community service. Your options: roadside cleanup, graffiti abatement, sanitation detail, or volunteer support at Knowland Park."

Paul blinked. "The zoo?"

The officer shrugged. "They always need help. Groundskeeping. Enclosure cleanup. It's dirty work."

Paul's mouth curled. "This is absurd. I've chaired committees—"

"Not anymore," the officer cut in. "You're an offender. You'll take the assignment, or the court will reconsider your sentence."

Paul leaned back, swallowing his pride like bile.

He noticed the officer's pen—chewed down, ink-stained fingers gripping it. A man doing his own kind of grunt work.

He almost respected it.

Almost.

The irony settled in: reduced to shoveling waste while his sister built an empire he no longer understood.

CHAPTER TWENTY

The Ballast Shift

* * *

BALLAST SHIFT — redistribution of weight that threatens stability.

* * *

The news feed played silently across the wall of her office: Paul Ellsworth leaving the courthouse, head lowered, hands empty. The crawl beneath his face read *Community service assigned. Assets under review.*

Mallory shut the screen off.

She didn't need the commentary. She already knew the story. She had written most of it.

In the beginning, she had only meant to shield him.

When the indictments came down and his allies scattered, it was Mallory who made the calls—quiet ones, to the right lawyers, the right collectors, the men who could make records vanish or reappear.

It was supposed to end when he was safe.

But safety had its own economy.

The first shipment she brokered wasn't art at all. A collector needed a crate flown in from Macau, no questions asked. Mallory knew the forms, the codes, the right customs officer to nudge.

It felt cleaner than selling a painting.

Easier than asking for another favor.

By the third shipment, she was the one giving orders.

He didn't understand that yet.

He wanted the old world back—the dinners, the donors, the city's applause. He still believed money came from shaking hands and saying the right things.

He didn't see where power actually lived.

In paperwork.

In bills of lading.

In warehouse manifests.

In what no one thought to question.

She had kept him close because she had to. The last time she let him drift, he nearly buried them both.

Distance was danger.

Her phone buzzed. A message from a contact at the port:

*The new manifest's clean. Shipment clears tonight. *

Mallory allowed herself a small smile.

The system was working.

As it should.

She thought of the old days—of Paul insisting he didn't need her.

He had called her cruel.

Maybe she was.

But cruelty had kept him alive.

She poured a glass of scotch and stared out at the Bay, cranes lifting containers in slow, measured rhythm.

CHAPTER TWENTY-ONE

The Hold Below

* * *

HOLD — the interior compartment where cargo is stored.

* * *

Port of Oakland – 12:30am

The truck rolled through the Port of Oakland gates after midnight, empty but waiting.

Ellsworth sat rigid in the passenger seat, diesel thick in his nose, the cranes casting hard light across everything. Up close, they looked different—not symbols, but machines. Massive. Indifferent.

He had once signed contracts that praised their efficiency.

Now he sat beneath them.

Watching how the work really happened.

At the guardhouse, Rudy—the inside man—leaned against the wall, cap low. Ellsworth climbed down from the cab, the envelope tucked into his coat.

Rudy's eyes flicked once to the cash before he slid it into his jacket.

"Manifest says you're empty," Rudy muttered. "You'll leave loaded. Logs won't show anything unusual."

At the gate, another agent waited. Another envelope changed hands. The scanner chirped. Clearance granted.

No eye contact.

Safer that way.

They rolled deeper into the yard. Men in headlamps moved like shadows, cracking open a container, sliding boxes down steel ramps into the truck.

Handbags. Electronics. Watches. All of it disappearing into the dark.

Ellsworth stayed close to the driver, careful not to draw attention. Still, one dockworker spotted him.

"Hey—where's your vest? Hardhat?" The voice cut sharp through the noise.

For a moment, Ellsworth froze.

He had worn tailored suits to council meetings. Silk ties to backroom deals.

Out here, he looked like what he was.

An outsider.

"Leave it," Rudy snapped, stepping between them. He pointed toward the far end of the yard, where warning strobes flashed. "They need you over there."

The dockworker cursed and jogged off.

Ellsworth's pulse slowed, though his palms were slick.

When the truck was loaded, they pulled out.

Ellsworth kept his eyes on the cranes receding in the mirror—steel giants frozen mid-motion, like gods who didn't care who stole beneath them.

Back at the warehouse, he walked the rows alone.

Mallory wasn't there. She didn't need to be.

He moved through the space with his hands behind his back, mimicking her posture without realizing it.

The auction room stood half-assembled—velvet ropes waiting to be strung, crates stacked beside the stage. A statue under cloth. Handbags in rows. Watches ticking faintly in the stillness.

Ellsworth paused in the doorway.

Memory dragged him backward.

Cinderblock walls. Metal doors slamming. Time thick and shapeless. He had told himself he was above it.

He hadn't been.

He had been just another inmate.

He kept that lesson now.

Tonight, he had nearly been caught by a man who saw too much.

He hated the feeling. But he understood it.

If he wanted back in the game, he would have to move carefully.

He rested his hand on the velvet rope, flexing his fingers until the tremor eased.

Mallory thought she was still shaping him. Still placing him.

He would let her.

For now.

But he would never go back inside. Not ever.

CHAPTER TWENTY-TWO

Full Ahead

* * *

FULL AHEAD — to move forward at maximum speed.

* * *

The memory came unbidden, sharp as a blade.

He was twelve. Mallory was sixteen, newly holding a learner's permit.

"Come on," she said, dangling the keys. "It'll be practice. You sit in the passenger seat. No one has to know."

Paul hesitated.

Mallory never asked twice.

She ordered.

The old Buick rattled down their street, Mallory's hands tight on the wheel, her grin too wide to trust. When she swerved to avoid a trash can, the fender clipped a mailbox and splintered it into the gutter.

The crack echoed down the block.

She slammed on the brakes. “Get out.”

Paul stared at her. “What?”

“Get out,” she repeated, sharper. “When the neighbors ask, you were driving. I was teaching you. You panicked and swerved. It’ll sound better.”

His mouth went dry.

Her hand clamped around his wrist, nails biting. “Say it. Or I tell Mom you begged me to drive. You want to be the little brother who wrecked the car and lied about it?”

When the neighbors came running, Mallory was already composed, her arm draped over his shoulders.

“He’s learning,” she said smoothly. “It was just an accident.”

Paul nodded, the words spilling out exactly as she had shaped them.

He took the blame.

Mallory never broke things.

She broke people.

* * *

Late morning, Knowland Park Zoo

The memory collapsed, replaced by the sour stink of mud and waste.

Ellsworth stood in the zoo pen, tugging at the sleeve of borrowed coveralls—one size too large, the fabric stiff, cuffs dragging over his wrists. His Italian loafers, once polished, were now soaked through, leather darkened and warped with every step.

A handler pointed with a shovel. "Start at the far end. Clear the piles, rake the hay. Watch your footing. Elephants don't care what you're wearing."

The stall smelled of rot and damp straw. A low groan rolled through the enclosure as the elephant shifted, deep enough to rattle his ribs.

He gripped the shovel like it was proof of his sentence.

"Keep it moving," the handler called, already walking away.

Ellsworth muttered under his breath. "I kept this city running. Zoning, permits, commerce—and now I shovel dung."

He swung too hard, scattering straw instead of lifting it. The elephant turned its head, unimpressed.

"Unbelievable," he hissed. "Thirty years of service, and this is what I get. Community redemption."

"First day?"

The voice caught him off guard.

He turned.

A woman stood at the far end of the enclosure, tone light, almost polite. A badge hung from her vest: U.S. Fish and Wildlife Service.

Ellsworth straightened immediately. "Volunteer program."

She nodded. "Uh-huh." Her eyes moved over him—shoes, cuffs, posture—cataloging. "You might want boots next time."

He said nothing.

She smiled faintly and walked on.

Later, at her clipboard, Clare Hinton made a note:

Ellsworth, Paul — volunteer. Possible city connection. Verify.

She hesitated, pen tapping once.

The name tugged at something—a headline, a hearing, a scandal.

The elephant trumpeted, sharp and sudden. Ellsworth flinched.

Clare glanced back just long enough to see him muttering under his breath.

She added another line:

not suited to public service.

At the edge of the enclosure, half-hidden in shade, a woman stood watching.

She watched Clare question Paul Ellsworth.

Watched the notes go onto the clipboard.

Watched Ellsworth curse at the work in front of him.

When she turned to leave, the sun caught the brass key at her throat, catching the light, a signal no one else seemed to see. Then she was gone.

CHAPTER TWENTY-THREE

The Pressure Line

* * *

PRESSURE LINE — depth where water exerts maximum force on a hull.

* * *

That night Mallory took him to the cellar. From the street, it passed for an old jazz club tucked into an alley, its neon sign flickering red.

Below, smoke curled through the air, mingling with the bassline drifting down from the trio above. The room glowed in low light—men in tailored suits, women in silk and diamonds, crystal catching and scattering what little light there was.

Ellsworth had scrubbed himself raw, but the zoo clung to him.

It lingered beneath the cologne—sweat, hay, something sour he couldn't quite name.

Mallory noticed.

She always noticed.

Her nose wrinkled, just once.

"What's that smell?" she murmured, low enough for him alone.

His throat tightened.

He didn't answer.

Mallory rose and took the floor. Workers unveiled crates one by one—handbags, watches, art objects—while she presided with the ease of a hostess and the authority of a judge.

Bids snapped through the room in clipped bursts. Greed moved quietly—nods, glances, small lifts of a hand.

Ellsworth tallied numbers, pen scratching across the ledger.

But the zoo stayed with him—handlers laughing, shovel in his hands, elephants shifting in the dark.

Then the final lot.

A carved ivory elephant.

The room stilled—then surged.

The irony hit him hard. His humiliation, carved and polished, paraded in front of buyers who would never understand it.

The bids climbed.

Then a ripple at the back of the room.

A woman—dark hair, wide eyes—out of place.

She tried to disappear behind a pair of guests.

Too late.

Heads turned.

Mallory didn't pause. "Continue."

The auctioneer faltered, then recovered. The rhythm resumed.

But Ellsworth felt it. The crack.

The moment control slipped.

The woman froze when someone caught her arm. Then came the shout, chairs scraping, movement breaking the room open as she bolted.

Still, the bidding continued.

Minutes later, the gavel fell.

Sold.

Mallory closed the sale with a smile sharp enough to cut.

She didn't look at him.

* * *

On the drive back, Ellsworth snapped.

"You keep me shoveling filth by day and tallying your books by night. I kept this city afloat for decades."

Mallory barely reacted.

His anger was background noise.

Security wasn't.

"That girl should never have reached the floor," she said, almost to herself.

Then, to him:

"And look what happens when things slip."

Her voice stayed calm. Controlled. Final.

"You're not here because you deserve it, Paul. You're here because you're still useful."

A beat.

"Don't confuse the two."

The words settled into him, heavier than the stench he carried

CHAPTER TWENTY-FOUR

The Tidal Lock

* * *

TIDAL LOCK — chamber that controls water levels to allow vessels to pass between tides.

* * *

Paul Ellsworth had been told to observe.

To learn.

He hated it.

Standing at Mallory's shoulder like a junior clerk, nodding while she checked crates and issued orders.

But habit held.

He had built his career on spotting cracks.

And here—buried in routine—he found one.

Four trucks left the port.

Only three arrived.

Every crate here was logged, stacked, accounted for.

So where did the fourth go?

At first, he dismissed it.

Coincidence.

Then he watched again.

Same pattern.

Night after night.

Paul said nothing.

Something shifted.

Mallory believed she controlled everything.

She didn't.

Someone else was pulling threads.

Paul felt it. Possibility.

The next night, when the trucks rolled out, Paul followed.

Hands damp on the wheel.

Every block a chance to turn back.

He didn't.

He stayed a few car lengths behind until the fourth truck slowed at a light near the freeway onramp.

Wrong direction.

Paul pulled alongside and honked once.

Sharp.

The driver glanced over.

Paul gestured.

Pull over.

The kid shook his head.

Paul cut him off, forcing him to the curb.

He got out, yanked the door open.

"You're not going anywhere," he said, voice rougher than he intended, "until you tell me who you're working for."

The driver tried to push past.

Paul grabbed his arm.

Hard.

"Mallory thinks every crate runs through her," he said. "But I've been watching. Four out, three in."

The kid froze.

Paul leaned closer.

"You don't want me asking her where the fourth goes."

Silence.

Then, quieter:

"Introduce me."

Not a command.

Almost a plea.

"Now."

CHAPTER TWENTY-FIVE

The Scuttled Ship

* * *

SCUTTLED SHIP — a vessel deliberately sunk to prevent capture.

* * *

In a back room above a pool hall in West Oakland, Ray Molina leaned against the window, the glow of his burner phone lighting his face.

The text was short:

Strike talk. Union might pull out soon.

Ray smirked. His inside man at the port was earning his keep.

With management distracted, Mallory distracted, everyone watching the picket lines instead of the gates, it was perfect cover.

He tapped out a reply with one thumb.

Keep listening. Don't get caught.

Then he slipped the phone away and turned back to his desk.

Let her have her auctions, Ray thought. The streets paid faster.

That night, Marty Butler brought Paul to a pool hall on San Pablo Avenue. Upstairs, the smell of cigarettes and spilled whiskey clung to the walls.

Ray Molina stood behind a battered desk, leather jacket creased at the elbows, his expression sharp but casual—the look of a man who had stumbled onto an angle and meant to squeeze it dry.

"So, you're the politician," Ray said, unimpressed. "The one playing apprentice to the lady in the peacoat."

Paul straightened his jacket, hiding the sweat at his collar. His pulse drummed, but his voice reached for steadiness.

"I know what's happening here. You're skimming her shipments. And you need someone who can give you cover while she's looking the other way."

Ray tilted his head, amused. "And you think that someone is you?"

Paul forced a smirk, though it felt brittle. "I don't have a choice. She keeps me on a leash. You let me in, I keep her blind, and maybe I get a leash of my own. We both win."

Ray studied him for a long beat, then cracked a smile.

"You've got stones, power broker. Desperate stones. That's useful."

He tapped ash into a tray and added, almost offhand, "Names you think are gone have a way of coming up again."

Paul frowned at that, but Ray was already extending his hand.

"Welcome to the sideshow."

Ray's grip was firm, cigarette smoke curling between them. Paul forced his own hand steady, though his pulse hammered.

As Ray let go, Paul's smirk slipped for half a breath.

This wasn't partnership.

It was survival.

A chance to hold something Mallory didn't know, couldn't control.

It wasn't about money.

It wasn't about power.

It was about proving, if only to himself, that he wasn't completely hers.

He locked the thought down before it could show on his face. In Mallory's world, secrets were currency.

And since his release, Paul had one of his own.

Ray lit another cigarette and leaned back in his chair.

"You know I'm taking a cut off the top."

Paul didn't blink. "I know you're taking more than Mallory thinks. And I know if she finds out, it won't be your head on the block first. It'll be mine, for keeping quiet."

Ray exhaled smoke, unfazed. Then he reached into the desk drawer and slid a thick envelope across the scarred wood.

"Consider it a finder's fee. You keep smiling for the lady in the peacoat, keep your mouth shut, and stay out of my trucks. Everybody wins."

Paul thumbed the edge of the bills, his smile thin and tight. "For now."

Ray grinned. "For now."

Paul tucked the envelope away. Not trust. Not partnership. Just the smallest crack of daylight between him and Mallory.

He told himself it was enough.

* * *

The next morning, Paul was back at Knowland Park Zoo, shoveling dung in borrowed coveralls while elephants trumpeted behind him. A teenager signed his timesheet with a flourish that made him grit his teeth.

From there, he went straight to Mallory's warehouse, ready to stand at her shoulder and nod while she tallied crates.

Two lives. Two masks. Two lies.

And both paying him—

for now.

CHAPTER TWENTY-SIX

The Lead Line

* * *

LEAD LINE — weighted line used to measure depth beneath a vessel.

* * *

It was late Wednesday night. Outside, the streets were quiet. Most of the crew had gone hours earlier, but inside Mallory's warehouse the lights still burned bright.

Half the cavernous space had been transformed into a Roaring Twenties fantasy: velvet drapes masking concrete walls, Art Deco lamps glowing gold, mirrored trays of champagne moving between guests in pearls and tuxedos. A jazz trio sawed through a brassy tune while Edison bulbs flickered overhead against the exposed beams.

At the front, a small stage displayed the evening's prizes. A string of pearls said to have once belonged to a Hollywood starlet.

A diamond-studded cigarette case rumored to have come through Havana. An antique gramophone with its horn polished to a trumpet's shine.

The bidders sipped champagne and raised numbered paddles with languid ease.

Mallory glided through it all, her sequined gown catching the light like a moving constellation. She paused only to murmur instructions, her gloved hand never still.

"Paul," she said without looking at him, "have the crew bring up the next crates. The brass fixtures and the silver cocktail shakers. And keep an eye on the back doors. Last time one of the porters nearly wandered where he shouldn't."

Paul forced a smile and dipped his head as though grateful for the task. He fetched. He waved. He nodded.

Until the bourbon in his hand became the only thing anchoring him.

Each trip back into the crowd left him feeling smaller, a servant in Mallory's glittering playhouse.

The laughter swelled as the night deepened. He knew it came from the auction floor—a bid won, a joke told—but bourbon made it cruel. Every chuckle bent toward him. Every raised glass became a finger pointing.

He drained another.

Then another.

That was when the voice cut through.

"Mister Ellsworth."

Paul turned, unsteady.

Mason Robbins stood there, cheeks flushed with liquor, tie crooked, wife on his arm glittering with diamonds. She was laughing at something Mallory had said moments earlier, leaning in like an old friend.

"Didn't think I'd see you here," Paul managed.

Robbins smirked. "My wife drags me to these things. She and Mallory are thick as thieves. Me? I come to keep her from bleeding me dry."

He leaned closer, wine sour on his breath.

"Though truth is, you already did most of the bleeding. Half my holdings sank the day they hauled you off in cuffs. You stink of failure, Ellsworth. And worse—"

He wrinkled his nose and stepped back.

"—you just plain stink."

The words landed harder than the bourbon.

Robbins tugged his wife away, disappearing into the tide of laughter and applause.

Paul stood rooted, glass empty, every laugh in the hall now a sneer, every whisper another finger pointed his way.

He slipped out into the night before the room could swallow him whole.

* * *

The car wove through Rockridge, bourbon thick in his veins. Campaign posters clung to storefronts and telephone poles, Ben Cooper's name glowing in the sodium light.

Cooper. Cooper. Cooper.

Every corner spat it back at him.

Then one loomed above the street, larger than the rest: a billboard with Ben's face smiling down, the words Integrity. Accountability. Change. stretched across the night sky.

Paul barked a laugh that curdled into a shout.

"Integrity? Accountability? You're nothing, Cooper! A clerk with a stack of papers and a loud mouth. You think you can carry a city?"

He pounded the steering wheel, voice rising.

"You're a fraud, and they're too blind to see it!"

He drove on, tires squealing, fury boiling as the billboard grin followed him in the rearview mirror.

The car carried him, as if by instinct, to the zoo.

The elephants stirred in their pens beneath the moonlight, massive shapes shifting in the dark. Paul leaned against the rail, voice gone raw.

"Inmates," he spat. "That's all you are. Caged. Forgotten. Just like me."

He hurled the words at them until his voice cracked.

The neighborhood lay still, porch lamps glowing behind drawn curtains. It was past midnight when he parked down the block from Mason Robbins's house.

Minutes later, he backed into the driveway, popped the trunk, dumped a steaming heap of dung across the concrete, struck a match, and watched the smoke curl into the night.

CHAPTER TWENTY-SEVEN

Contraband Currents

* * *

CONTRABAND CURRENTS — unofficial flows of goods moved outside regulation.

* * *

"Preliminary reports out of Customs," Clare's supervisor said, pacing before the conference table. "We've got unregistered ivory fragments showing up in Port of Oakland containers. Someone's moving carved pieces through import channels and laundering them through local auctions—high-end buyers, maybe an underground fence."

Clare's pen hovered above her notebook.

Oakland. Ivory. Auctions.

Her mind flashed to the alley, the jazz club, the woman running.

I knew it.

The supervisor continued. "Fish and Wildlife will coordinate with Homeland Security, but keep your eyes open in your existing facilities—anywhere carved ivory could hide in plain sight."

Clare nodded, heart hammering. She said nothing about the photos she'd taken outside the Pink Lady. Nothing about the woman she had chased through the tunnel.

When the meeting broke, she lingered by the door.

The threads aligned too neatly to ignore. That volunteer—Ellsworth—the name she had written down at the zoo. She remembered his slick shoes in the hay, the muttering, the air of a man convinced he was above the work.

Coincidence? Maybe.

Her gut said otherwise.

Without sharing what she knew, Clare slipped out, phone already in hand.

She typed Paul Ellsworth Oakland into the search bar.

Headlines flooded the screen:

City Power Broker Convicted — Sentenced to Community Service

A familiar face stared back at her, hollow-eyed beneath courthouse lights.

She closed the browser and headed for the parking lot.

If he's mixed up in this, I'll find out myself.

* * *

Later that afternoon, Paul dragged himself back to the zoo. His shirt was wrinkled, his collar stained, and the sour tang of bourbon clung to him like a second skin. He hadn't shaved. His eyes bloodshot, his hair plastered with sweat.

The primates noticed first.

As he shuffled past their enclosure, a chorus of hoots and rattles followed him, sharp and mocking. He imagined their jeers were the same laughter that had driven him from Mallory's party.

The elephants caught his scent as he approached their pen. Both shifted uneasily, trunks lifting, ears flaring. One gave a deep, rumbling chuff that reverberated through his chest. The other stamped a foot, kicking up dust.

Each sound landed like an indictment.

He muttered back at them while he shoveled listlessly, dung piling unevenly, sweat dripping into his eyes. He knew he was doing bad work, but his arms felt heavy as lead and his stomach rolled.

By the time he dragged the wheelbarrow away, his coveralls reeked worse than his breath.

The volunteer coordinator waited by the gate, clipboard in hand. A young woman with a neat ponytail, she gave him a once-over, nose wrinkling.

"Mr. Ellsworth," she said flatly, "your appearance is not acceptable, and your work today was barely passable. If you're serious about completing your service, you need to show up on time, sober, and ready to work. Next time, I won't sign this."

She scrawled her signature across the timesheet with one hard flick and handed it back.

"Shape up, or you're done."

Paul stuffed the sheet into his pocket, head lowered, throat dry. The animals' stares seemed to follow him as he left, the monkeys still hooting behind him.

* * *

That night, Ray called Paul into the back office of the shuttered pool hall. Smoke curled in the air, blue light pooling across the felt tables.

Ray leaned against the wall, voice low.

"Get the kid out. He's not safe walking around. He'll fold under real questioning. You're going to keep a lid on him."

Paul frowned. "Why me? You should handle your own mess."

Ray's eyes hardened.

"It is my mess. And I need you to help me clean it up."

He stepped forward.

"Thomas Forrester got me fired from the port. I had a good job before he tanked my certification. Said I was reckless. Said I couldn't be trusted. Signed the paper that blacklisted me. I had that job for three years before the container incident. One bad day, and he put his name on my termination papers."

He spat the words like they burned.

"Now it's his turn to feel what that's like. Cost of doing business."

Paul felt the name land.

Forrester.

He wasn't sure yet how it connected, but this was his chance to earn Ray's trust. And if Ray owed him, maybe that debt could stand between him and Mallory one day.

Paul gave a short nod. "Fine. I'll handle it."

* * *

At a quiet bail window on Jackson Street, one of Ray's warehouse men slid paperwork across the counter while Paul stood a step back, collar turned up.

Hours later, Marty Butler shuffled out, shoulders hunched, eyes darting as if he expected the cuffs to snap back around his wrists at any moment.

"I did exactly what Ray told me to do," Marty whispered.

Paul silenced him with a look. "Then you keep quiet. You've already said enough. Anything more, and you're finished."

That night, Paul drove Marty through the gates of his estate.

The kid's eyes widened at the long drive and the hollow grandeur of the place.

"This is yours?"

"Yes," Paul muttered. "What's left of it."

The awe drained from Marty's face when Paul led him down the narrow basement stairwell. Concrete walls pressed close on either side, the air cooler, heavier.

At the end of the hall stood a plain door. Paul swung it open to reveal a furnished room—a bed neatly made, a small bathroom in the corner, a single lamp casting thin light.

"You stay here," Paul said. "You have what you need. Food and water when I decide. No phone. No visitors. No wandering."

Marty opened his mouth to protest, but Paul had already snatched the phone from his hand. The motion was quick. Final.

The door shut.

The lock turned with a metallic snap.

Paul lingered on the other side, hand still on the key. For a moment he was back in jail, hearing metal doors slam, feeling the silence thicken around him, watching a man shrink when freedom was taken away.

His smirk faltered.

What rose in its place felt closer to dread.

He pocketed the key and walked away, leaving Marty to the quiet he knew too well.

It wasn't Santa Rita that made this familiar.

That memory belonged to childhood.

* * *

Four years younger, he had lived under Mallory's rule more than their parents'. They worked long hours running the family business, leaving her in charge. She had been clever even then, sharper than anyone gave her credit for—a smart student with a way of bending teachers, neighbors, and most of all Paul to her will.

He remembered being eleven, her voice low and certain as she pushed him into the basement closet.

Do what I say, or stay in the dark all day.

He could still feel the musty air, the silence pressing in, the scrape of her shoes as she walked away.

Age had not changed that pattern. As a young widow, she had married up, securing money and access to rooms Paul could only dream of entering. College had been his first taste of freedom, but even then she reeled him back in—pulling strings for his first job, shaping what he would say, how he would act. He told himself he had earned it. In truth, Mallory had placed him like a chess piece.

The money had made up for the reach she had into his life.

Or so he thought.

His estate had been the one fortress he believed she could not touch.

Now, as he locked another man away, the truth gnawed at him.

He was repeating her ways.

Becoming her.

A thought sparked and vanished before he could smother it:

If the only way out was to defy her, could he do it?

CHAPTER TWENTY-EIGHT

The Breakwater

* * *

BREAKWATER — built to protect a harbor from the open sea.

* * *

Mallory's office smelled faintly of smoke and old wood. Paul sat stiff in the leather chair, the zoo's stench still clinging to his ruined loafers.

One of Mallory's men slipped inside, cap in hand.

"About the situation at the Pink Lady that night. The woman who was snooping—we checked the camera footage. We got a license plate and a name."

Mallory's expression didn't change, but her gloved fingers curled against the armrest.

"Well?" she said. "Are you going to tell me?"

The man nodded. "Maya Forrester."

Mallory dismissed him with a tilt of her hand. When the door closed, her gaze lingered on the paneled wall as though she could see through it.

"Loose ends are dangerous," she said at last, voice low and sharp. "Questions unravel everything."

Paul shifted in his seat, throat dry. "Probably just a kid trying to prove something."

But the name had already lodged in him like a thorn. Forrester. Ray had made his grudge clear. Marty had repeated it. Now it pressed on him from all sides.

Beneath that sat another unease:

Marty Butler, locked in his basement, a secret even Mallory did not know he was keeping.

If she ever connected the two, she would see at once that he had worked behind her back.

Mallory's gaze snapped toward him. "You're quiet tonight, Paul. I don't care for quiet men."

He forced a smile that never reached his eyes. "Just thinking about the next auction. The speakeasy worked, but it was exposed. Too many people close enough to start wondering."

Mallory arched a brow. "And?"

The answer came out faster than he meant it to.

"Knowland Park. The zoo. After hours. I know the gates, the service roads, blind corners. If the paperwork looks clean, nobody questions trucks out there. It's secure. It's exclusive. Your clients would never forget it."

Silence stretched. His pulse rose with it.

Then Mallory smiled.

Sharp. Approving.

"Not just an auction," she said softly. "A masquerade. Safari theme. Masks, champagne, wealth pretending it's wild for a night. They'll pay twice as much for the story as for the lots."

Paul swallowed, relief loosening his chest. For once, she liked his idea. For once, he mattered.

But her earlier words clung like smoke.

Loose ends are dangerous.

His mind snagged again on Forrester, on Marty, on everything he was hiding. The elephants at the zoo felt less like animals now than judges waiting in the dark.

Mallory's smile still lingered in his mind when he left her office—sharp, approving, dangerous. She liked his idea. She would turn it into a spectacle.

For a moment, he almost believed that meant he was safe.

* * *

That night, at the far end of his hollow estate, Paul unlocked the basement door. The air inside was cool and stale. Marty Butler sat hunched on the edge of the bed, eyes rimmed red, hands working restlessly against each other.

Paul set a bag of fast food and bottled water on the table, then pocketed the key again.

"Eat. Drink. Stay quiet. That's the deal."

Marty's voice came out hoarse. "How long are you keeping me here?"

Paul paused. Considered.

"As long as it takes to keep me safe."

Behind him, the bolt slid home with a sound too much like Santa Rita.

And in the dark, Mallory's words rang again:

Loose ends are dangerous.

CHAPTER TWENTY-NINE

Storm Glass

* * *

STORM GLASS — instrument used to predict approaching weather.

* * *

The interrogation room was concrete, silence, and the low hum of a single fluorescent light overhead. Ray Molina sat across from Detectives Alvarez and Chen, his leather jacket folded on the table, an unlit cigarette rolling between his fingers.

Alvarez leaned back in his chair, unimpressed.

"You've been running games around this port a long time, Molina. Fish and Wildlife is already sniffing around for contraband shipments. You think we don't see it?"

Ray smirked. "Then prove it."

Chen slid a folder across the table, its notes marked in yellow.

"We've got patterns. Containers logged in, never logged out. Goods gone missing. And we've got witnesses—your own boys, caught moving things that didn't belong to them. They all say the same name."

Ray closed his eyes.

Alvarez leaned forward, voice sharpening.

"Here's the deal. You're looking at conspiracy, theft, maybe racketeering. That's years in San Quentin. Or you talk. Tell us who's really pulling the strings, and maybe you walk."

Ray drummed his fingers on the table, buying time.

Mallory Thornton had power, reach, connections.

Prison had walls.

That was all.

At last, he let out a breath.

"All right. You want names? It's not just me. It's her. Mallory Thornton. She's the one running the auctions. Her brother Paul's in it too, playing lapdog, pretending he's still somebody. They move goods through a warehouse in West Oakland. That's your hub."

Chen's pen stilled. "Auctions?"

Ray shrugged. "Black-market shows. Velvet ropes. Rich people bidding on stolen goods. You put someone in that warehouse; you'll see it yourself."

Alvarez's gaze sharpened. "And Paul? What's his angle?"

Ray leaned back, lips curling. "Desperate. Wants back what he lost. But he's sloppy. "Word is, he grabbed one of my guys—Marty Butler. Kid got caught in the mess." I think he's got him stashed at his estate. Wouldn't surprise me if the kid's locked in a basement right now."

The room went still.

Chen closed his notebook. "You're ready to testify to all of it? Mallory Thornton, Paul Ellsworth, the warehouse, the auctions, and Butler?"

Ray nodded once. "With immunity. I'm not doing time for their game."

Alvarez stood, gathering the folder. "You'll get your deal. But understand this, Molina—once you give us their world, you don't get to live in it anymore."

Ray sucked his teeth and sighed. "Wouldn't be the first time I walked away."

PART III

CHAPTER THIRTY

Bravo Zulu

* * *

BRAVO ZULU — a naval signal meaning "well done."

* * *

October 2007

The house in Vallejo felt warmer than it had in weeks—like something heavy had finally lifted.

The storm of Thomas's arrest, the endless churn of lawyers and union turmoil, had finally broken just enough for him to breathe again.

Maya set her bag on the chair and grinned across the kitchen table. "It's over, Mom. We figured it out. Dad's clear."

Doris pressed a hand to her mouth, eyes brimming. She pulled Thomas into a hug so tight it startled him, then wrapped her arms around Maya, too. "You found the proof?"

Maya nodded, her voice alive with conviction. "The manifests, the discrepancies — all of it. The detectives have the evidence now. They know Dad was framed, and they know who did it."

"You gave them the truth they needed to see," Thomas said. "That's what got me out from under it."

He paused.

"They're still looking for Butler. Which means this isn't over. But I'm not their focus anymore."

Doris's relief spilled into laughter, light and unrestrained. She cupped Maya's face, studying her. "Look at you. Eyes shining like I haven't seen in years. You've found something, haven't you? Something that's yours."

Maya hesitated. "I just... wanted to help Dad."

Doris shook her head gently. "No, more than that. You chased the truth when no one else could see it. Maybe this isn't something you stumbled into, Maya. Maybe it's who you are."

Maya had no answer — only the flicker of possibility curling through her chest.

At the far end of the table, Skip set down his glass with a thud. "Glad the mess is settled. But the damn strike's still strangling everything." He scowled, tugging at his ball cap. "Fleet Week starts tomorrow. It was supposed to be a celebration. Hard to cheer for parades when the port's dead."

Thomas chuckled. "Let them have their Blue Angels, Skip. The work will still be here when the smoke clears."

Skip grunted, then softened, turning toward his son-in-law. "I'll say this, Tom — I always knew you weren't guilty. Otherwise, I'd have court-martialed you myself."

The table broke into laughter, even Skip cracking a crooked grin. He pointed at Maya, pride glinting in his eyes. " Bravo Zulu, kid," he said, the old Navy phrase steady and sure. "Means 'well done.'"

Doris reached for Maya's hand, her smile tender. "Whatever comes next, you've proven you can stand in the storm. That's no small thing."

Maya squeezed back, her thoughts already moving ahead—past the kitchen, past the relief—toward the shadows still shifting beneath the cranes.

The work wasn't finished.

It had only just begun

CHAPTER THIRTY-ONE

Storm Warning

* * *

STORM WARNING — an official alert of approaching severe weather.

* * *

Oakland – 6:00pm

The warehouse hummed with preparation, but something in the rhythm was off.

Crates cracked open, items checked, then sealed again in tissue and velvet. Two men Paul didn't recognize moved among the crew—muscled, efficient, and not asking questions. He noticed them, frowned, but let it pass. There was too much work to question new hands.

By dusk, the trucks were rolling toward the zoo.

At Paul's estate, an unmarked sedan idled. Inside, a detective marked the time as Paul's car pulled through the gates.

He didn't miss the stop.

He didn't miss the return.

And he didn't miss the hesitation.

He watched Paul duck inside, then return minutes later.

Down in the basement, Marty sat on the edge of the mattress, eyes hollow. Paul slid in a bag of food and bottles of water. "Eat. Don't cause trouble."

"Why keep me here?" Marty said. "It's over."

Paul didn't answer. He locked the door, the bolt sliding home with a sound too much like Santa Rita. Upstairs, he adjusted his jacket and headed back out, unaware of the officer noting his every move.

More unaware still was the second car that followed him down the hill.

* * *

Oakland – 9:00pm

The Education Center at Knowland Park Zoo looked ordinary from the outside, its windows dark, its doors locked. Inside, temporary blackout screens ensured no light leaked into the night. Mallory's men flanked the entrance.

Guests arrived in chauffeured sedans that melted back into the city, leaving the lot empty and still.

Within, the transformation was stark: velvet-draped tables, hushed lighting, and displays of rare goods arranged for eager bidders. The air buzzed with champagne whispers and the muted clink of glasses.

Mallory glided through the room, her satin dress sweeping the floor, every flick of her gloved wrist drawing another bid.

At center stage, attendants unveiled a carved ivory tusk, its pale surface gleaming under the lamps. The room hushed, then stirred with hungry murmurs as the bidding began.

Excited murmurs swept the crowd, paddles shot up, numbers climbed. "Once in a lifetime," Mallory said smoothly, her voice carrying like silk over stone.

From outside, the elephants began to trumpet — low, resonant, then louder, their voices rising with the fever of the room.

Paul stood at the edge of the crowd, unease prickling his skin. Each blast cut sharper, echoing through the blacked-out walls. He excused himself, slipping down the path toward the enclosure.

The air was cool, damp with hay and earth. The elephants paced restlessly, their trunks raised, eyes catching the movement of figures beyond the glass.

"Quiet," Paul whispered, pressing against the fence. "
“Please,” he whispered. “Just—be quiet.”

The trumpeting only grew louder, reverberating in his chest. He gripped the bars, useless, desperate.

And there it was — the clarity he had been avoiding. He was keeping a man locked in his basement, standing in filth to keep his sister's secrets, and now shushing elephants enraged by the sale of their own kind's bones.

The thought came without permission.

What the hell am I doing?

The question hollowed him. The smirk he always forced, the false confidence, all of it drained away until he was just a man clinging to bars in the dark.

* * *

Across town, outside Paul's estate—the net tightened.

Two detectives emerged from an unmarked car. Weapons ready. They breached the side door, sweeping room by room until they reached the basement.

The lock gave way. Marty Butler, the same young dockworker who had named Forrester under Ray's pressure, now blinked into the light, terrified and trembling. He flinched, then broke down with relief as hands pulled him out, voices promising safety.

* * *

Back at Knowland Park, the undercover men moved into place. A signal passed. The power surged. The room exploded with sound.

Lights snapped on.

Music cut mid-note.

The room fractured.

"Police! Stay where you are!"

Paddles clattered to the floor.

Guests screamed and ran for the door. Mallory's mask never slipped; she was already moving, voice snapping at her crew even as officers poured in through every entrance.

Paul pressed himself against the bars, the elephants trumpeting so loud it felt like the earth itself was calling judgment. Sirens wailed outside. Boots thundered.

The raid had come, and Clare Hinton entered with the federal team, badge ready—Fish and Wildlife, supporting jurisdiction.

Chaos ripped through the education center. Guests bolted. Masks slipping. Jewelry clutched in trembling hands. Officers in plain clothes shed their disguises. Weapons raised, corralling bidders toward the walls.

Mallory moved like tide through wreckage, silent and sure. She managed to find her way outdoors.

The two undercover men saw the movement—but a surge of panicked bidders crashed between them, chairs splintering, bodies colliding.

"Paul!" she hissed.

He tore himself from the bars of the elephant enclosure and stumbled back toward her. For a breath, he thought she might let herself be cornered — but then her eyes met his, cold and calculating.

"This way."

She shoved him toward a service door at the rear. The two undercover men saw movement but were swept aside by panicked bidders crashing through chairs and tables.

By the time they regained line of sight, Mallory and Paul had vanished into the night—and a single Fish and Wildlife officer was already moving through the wreckage, camera flashing.

Clare Hinton logged every detail: the ivory crates, the broken glass, the empty ledger still warm from a man's hand. Her evidence would hold, the seizure complete, jurisdiction clean.

But as the uniforms took over, she lingered near the alley longer than she should have, telling herself her part was done. Yet the questions remained.

She closed her notebook.

The case was over.

But something about it didn't feel finished.

CHAPTER THIRTY-TWO

The Muster

* * *

MUSTER — gathering of crew before duty.

* * *

The café on the waterfront buzzed with late-morning chatter, the smell of coffee and griddled pancakes drifting through the air.

Maya slid a folded newspaper across the table. The headline screamed in bold: ILLEGAL AUCTION RAIDED — POLICE SEIZE MILLIONS IN CONTRABAND.

The photo beneath the headline showed a blurred figure being led out in cuffs. Not Mallory. Not Paul

Rich let out a low whistle. "Unbelievable. Paul Ellsworth, tied into this whole mess. And his sister—Mallory Thornton—turns out to be the real muscle behind the curtain."

Fiona stirred her tea, her eyes sharp. "Mallory Thornton. Now people will know that name."

"And yours," Ben said. "They might not print it, but that doesn't matter what the article says. You know what you did." You and your dad gave them what they needed to break the case open."

Maya shrugged, but there was pride in her eyes. "We followed the gaps. Once we proved the records were falsified, the rest fell into place. Dad's name is clear. The operation isn't."

Rich smiled. "You make it sound easy."

"It wasn't," Maya said quietly. "But it's not finished."

Fiona lifted her cup in salute. "Here's to doing the work that matters."

Ben chuckled, leaning back. "Speaking of names, I can't walk two blocks without seeing Cooper somewhere."

Rich raised his mug. "See? You're already trending higher than Ellsworth."

Fiona scoffed playfully. "And both of you better be registered to vote by Election Day—which, might I remind you, is right after Fleet Week."

Ben grinned. "You'll be the first to make sure of it."

Maya smiled. "And I'll make sure it counts. Now, about Skipper's ceremony tomorrow—we're leaving from Vallejo by ferry. The ship's the USS Bonhomme Richard. After the honoring there'll be food and photos, so wear your best sailor suit. Let's make it festive."

Their laughter rose, a welcome relief after weeks of carrying heavy loads. For a moment, the weight lifted.

Then Ben's expression sobered. "There's still the problem we can't shake. Ellsworth and his sister vanished during the raid. No one knows where they are."

Maya leaned forward, her resolve hardening. "Tomorrow is for Skipper. Whatever they try next, we'll face it together."

Outside, the Bay shimmered under the sun. Across the water, San Francisco's skyline waited—Fleet Week banners already unfurled, promising celebration while two dangerous figures were still out there—unaccounted for.

CHAPTER THIRTY-THREE

Deep Channel

* * *

DEEP CHANNEL — deepest navigable passage in a waterway.

* * *

Her supervisor called it a "textbook operation," and even the regional director had stopped by her cubicle to shake her hand. Clare Hinton smiled through the congratulations, the flash of the camera, the promise of commendations. For once, she let herself enjoy it. After years of chasing paperwork, she had broken a case that mattered.

By evening, the adrenaline had softened into glow. The women from her building had brought wine and pie for their Thursday book club, claiming they couldn't wait to "hear it from the source."

They met in Clare's apartment this time—a habit born of her good lighting and her knack for hospitality.

"Come on," Lisa said, topping off everyone's glass. "You're not going to make us wait until dessert, are you? Tell us how it really went down."

Clare smiled, feigning reluctance. "It was mostly coordination—undercover agents, timing, the usual chaos. But we did recover more than a dozen carved tusks and artifacts. The auction was happening right under everyone's nose."

The group gasped and murmured, leaning in. "Were there arrests?" someone asked.

"Some," Clare said carefully. "Others...slipped away. But we'll find them."

Lisa grinned. "See, I told you she was the real deal. Not like those TV detectives—you actually do the work."

Laughter circled the table, soft and approving. Clare basked in it for a moment, savoring the warmth of being seen, of being right.

Then Lisa tilted her head. "Hey, whatever happened with that girl you mentioned before? The one you said might've been involved?"

Clare's smile faltered. "Oh. That."

"Did she ever turn up?" Lisa pressed, sipping her wine. "You seemed convinced she was part of it."

Clare hesitated. The image flashed unbidden—the young woman sprinting from the alley, terrified, not calculating.

Maya.

In all the reports and confiscated evidence, not one mention of her name. Had she misread everything from the start?

“She’s not in the file,” Clare said. "Maybe she was just in the wrong place."

Lisa laughed. "Or maybe you scared her off. You're scarier than you think, Clare-Bear."

The room filled again with easy chatter, glasses clinking, pages turning. But Clare's thoughts had already drifted back to the alley, to the look on the girl's face, to the unanswered why still humming at the edge of memory.

She told herself she'd moved on. She'd done her job, earned her praise. Still, standing by the window later, watching distant lights ripple across the dark water, she caught herself whispering, “I was right,” she whispered.

“I had to be.”

CHAPTER THIRTY-FOUR

The Wake

* * *

WAKE — the trail of disturbed water left behind a moving vessel.

* * *

Alameda - midday

The yacht rocked gently on the water, Harbor Bay lapping against its hull. Its name, painted in gaudy script across the stern, was a cruel joke: The Alibi.

Below deck, the air was close and stale with diesel and salt. Mallory paced the narrow cabin, sneakers scuffing against the boards, her hair pulled back, her satin and gloves traded for shorts and a plain shirt. Even stripped of her polish, her anger made the space feel smaller.

Paul sat hunched on the built-in bench, trousers still streaked with dirt, shoes crusted from the elephant pen. The stink of hay and waste clung to him.

Mallory stopped and faced him, her voice sharp enough to cut. "Do you realize what you've done? My operation — years of work, contacts, clients — burned to the ground. Because of you. The zoo, of all places. The zoo. You turned it into a circus, and now everything is ash."

Paul lifted his head, eyes red-rimmed. "I—"

"No," she snapped, slicing the word across him. "Answer me this: why did you have a man locked in your basement?"

His throat worked. "Ray wanted him gone."

Mallory froze. "Ray?"

Paul nodded. "Ray Molina. He was stealing from you. Four trucks left the port, only three came to you. I saw it. I followed the fourth. That's where I found him." He made me a deal. Said if I kept you blind, he'd make sure I got a cut. I was desperate. I thought I could finally have something that wasn't yours."

Mallory's expression hardened, fury radiating. She didn't care who this 'Molina' was. What enraged her was not the name but the betrayal.

"You were working an angle. Against me. While parading as my right hand."

Paul's voice cracked. "When Butler was arrested, "Ray told him to name Forrester as the fall guy." But if Marty talked again, it would all unravel. Ray told me to keep him quiet, so I did. That's why he was in my basement."

The name landed heavy. "Forrester."

Mallory's eyes narrowed. "Forrester? Maya Forrester was the girl at the Pink Lady."

Paul blinked. "Her father?"

Mallory laughed, a sound sharp and hollow.

"Maya Forrester," Mallory repeated.
"She was in Cooper's circle. In that courtroom. Then she shows up at my auction."

A beat.

"And now you're telling me her father is the man your dock rat tried to bury?"

Paul's mind reeled. Maya — the same woman tied to Cooper, the same Cooper whose signs covered every corner of Oakland. The lines blurred until they knotted tight around his throat.

Mallory stepped closer, her face inches from his. "You betrayed me. You ruined everything. And for what? To play petty games with thieves? You're finished, Paul. There's no crawling back from this."

He saw it clearly — her fury wasn't a storm to wait out. It was final.

Paul stared at the floorboards, knowing there was no path left that led back to his sister's side.

The Alibi rocked again in Harbor Bay, the water outside calm, mocking the storm inside.

Mallory straightened, her voice flat and lethal. "Then we make them pay," Mallory said.

Her eyes didn't leave him.

"Starting with Maya Forrester."

CHAPTER THIRTY-FIVE

Fleet Week

* * *

FLEET WEEK — an annual celebration honoring military service at port cities.

* * *

At midnight, word spread that the strike was over. Agreements were signed, the cranes were moving again. But the headlines hadn't changed.

Two suspects were still missing.

Morning came flawless—blue sky, flags snapping, brass bands striking up marches. The Vallejo ferry terminal thrummed with relief. Boats waited at the pier, decks polished, bunting fluttering red, white, and blue.

At the center stood the grandest of them all: the ferry that would carry them to San Francisco, leading the ceremonial procession toward the Fleet Week flagship, the USS Bonhomme Richard.

Captain Byron Harper stood tall in full regalia, his jacket pressed sharp, medals pinned to his chest, cap gleaming white in the sunlight. He looked every bit the man the city was there to honor. Doris beamed at his side, her hand resting proudly on his arm.

Maya adjusted his sash and whispered, "Perfect."

“Damn thing itches,” he muttered. “But I’ll wear it.” His eyes softened as he looked at her. "Wouldn't miss this moment."

Behind them, Rich mingled with Fiona and Ben, all dressed in their best. Thomas stood near Doris, smiling at his father-in-law with quiet pride. For once, no tension pressed on their shoulders. It was all about the music, laughter, and sunlight dancing on the Bay.

Fiona snapped a photo on her phone of Ben, already planning to send it out on campaign channels.

Ben grinned, a little embarrassed. "Don't make this about me."

Rich clapped him on the back and also lifted his camera to take a photo. "Too late. You're a big deal now."

The band struck louder, brass bright and defiant, the convoy horns echoing across the water. The day felt unshakable. The day felt unshakable.

As if nothing could touch them out here on the water.

CHAPTER THIRTY-SIX

The Drift

* * *

DRIFT — slow movement caused by wind or current rather than power.

* * *

The ferry was alive with movement. Coast Guard cutters, tugs, sailboats, excursion vessels, and the Blue & Gold Fleet catamarans slipping past one another under the sun. Even the Red & White fleet had a presence, offering cruises around the Bay. The water was a tapestry of traffic, engines humming, sails fluttering, horns echoing, mariners saluting the company of vessels lined in procession.

The convoy progressed, engines churning, horns sounding, people waving from piers. San Francisco's skyline glittered ahead; banners floated along the Embarcadero; the atmosphere was buoyant, triumphant.

Captain Harper straightened, puffed out his chest slightly, and lifted his cap as he waved to the crowd.

The family behind him snapped photos, exchanged smiles, and stood quietly in the glow of the celebration.

They approached the towering USS Bonhomme Richard, anchored and ready. Gangways lowered, flags snapped to full mast, and guests poured aboard with cheers.

The admiral's voice rang out, crisp over the speakers, honoring Captain Byron Harper for his 30 years of Navy service as a captain. When the admiral pinned the medal, applause rolled like surf. Doris embraced her father, Thomas's pride was quiet and deep, Maya's camera flashed, Rich and Ben stood shoulder to shoulder. For one moment everything felt redeemed.

But beyond the glow of flags and brass, Mallory Thornton's hunger for retribution was already coiling, poised to strike.

Maya and Rich walked along the promenade, hand in hand, both caught in the easy rhythm of celebration. Families lined the barricades, kids on shoulders, flags waving as the jets carved blue-white arcs across the sky.

Then Maya heard her name.

"Excuse me—Maya?"

She turned, startled. A woman stood a few paces away, half-hidden by the crowd. Blonde hair pinned neatly back, a badge flashed briefly before she tucked it away.

"I'm Clare Hinton," the woman said. "Fish and Wildlife Service."

Maya frowned. "Okay...?"

"We crossed paths once," Clare went on, voice tight but polite. "At the Pink Lady. You were there that night."

Maya's breath caught. "That was you?"

"Yes." Clare's tone softened. "I need to ask you something. Why were you there?"

Maya stared at her. "You followed me that night, didn't you?"

Clare hesitated. "I was observing—"

Maya cut her off. "And in the tunnel, too? That was you behind me?" Her voice dropped low, sharp. "You nearly got us both killed."

Clare blinked, startled. "I was only trying to understand what you were doing. You were there, connected to—"

Rich stepped between them, his expression dark. "Connected to what? Who are you?"

Clare lifted her hands slightly, trying to calm the moment. "It's not what you think. I was working a case. I thought you were involved."

Maya's tone iced over. "You had no right to follow me. You don't know what you're talking about."

Rich angled himself closer, a quiet shield between them. "You need to step back."

Clare opened her mouth, then closed it. Another roar from the sky swallowed her reply. The jets screamed overhead, contrails curling in the blue like handwriting on paper. The crowd cheered.

When the noise faded, Maya and Rich were already walking away, swallowed by the throng.

Clare stayed where she was, the sound of applause and laughter swelling around her, the smell of popcorn and salt in the air. For a moment she thought about calling after them—but the words stuck.

She'd wanted answers. Instead, she was left with silence and the uneasy realization that maybe she'd been the one who'd gone too far.

Clare turned toward the water, the noise of Fleet Week swelling back around her—

"He wasn't suited to public service."

The voice came from behind her.

Calm. Certain.

Clare froze.

She turned slowly.

The woman stood a few paces back, unremarkable in the crowd—dark jacket, ball cap, nothing that called attention.

But her eyes held steady.

Clare's pulse ticked up. "Excuse me?"

"That's what you wrote," the woman said.

A beat.

Clare's fingers tightened slightly at her side.

The clipboard. The pen. The enclosure.

She hadn't said it out loud.

She hadn't written it anywhere that mattered.

"Who are you?"

The woman ignored the question. Her gaze shifted briefly toward the crowd—toward where Maya and Rich had disappeared. Then back.

"If I were you," she said, "I'd keep my eye on the volunteer."

Clare frowned. "Ellsworth?"

The woman didn't confirm it.

She didn't need to.

She stepped back, already folding into the movement of the crowd.

"And Clare—"

Just enough to stop her.

"Give my regards to Marlowe."

Clare's breath caught.

She took a step forward. "Wait—"

But the woman was gone.

Swallowed by flags and laughter and the roar of jets overhead.

Clare stood still, her mind racing—not about the girl anymore, but about the note she never meant anyone to see.

CHAPTER THIRTY-SEVEN

Current Turns

* * *

CURRENT TURNS — the point at which the direction of flow reverses.

* * *

The sun melted into the Bay in a wash of orange and rose. The honored ferry cut a steady path home, as families leaned against the rails, weary but smiling.

Captain Harper sat straighter than usual, his medal gleaming against his jacket. Doris stayed close, her hand on his arm, her eyes still damp with pride.

Thomas leaned on the rail beside Ben, his voice low, carrying the rhythm of a man who had lived it all before. "I've seen my share of strikes, but this one nearly broke us. Glad it settled in time. Never easy. Not once in thirty years."

Ben nodded, rubbing his palms together absently. "I can believe it. I've been out knocking on doors and shaking hands every day. Thought it would be nothing compared to real work, but my palms are callused like I've been swinging a hammer. Different kind of labor, but it wears you down just the same."

Thomas gave him a sidelong glance, then a grunt of respect. "Hard work's hard work. Doesn't matter the tool."

Toward the stern, Rich and Maya sat shoulder to shoulder, wrapped under a blanket. Her head rested against his chest, his arm snug around her shoulders. They murmured to each other, laughing quietly, content.

Fiona stood apart, the wind tugged at her coat and made her braids lifting in the breeze. The lights of San Francisco glowed in the distance, for a beat she looked lost in the beauty of it, as if trying to hold the day still.

The ferry eased into Vallejo under a sky streaked with violet and gold, the day closing on peace.

For now.

CHAPTER THIRTY-EIGHT

The Undertow

* * *

UNDERTOW — a subsurface current pulling against the visible surface flow.

* * *

Vallejo – 7:00pm

Back at the Forrester house, the celebration lingered—jackets shed, shoes kicked off, voices spilling easy laughter.

Skipper was out of his uniform now, dressed down in his favorite track suit, medal tucked safely away. He looked as content as Doris had ever seen him, settled at the kitchen table with a steaming mug of coffee.

Doris brought out a red velvet cake, Skipper's favorite, its bright layers glowing as she cut generous slices. The kitchen filled with the sweet smell of cocoa and cream cheese frosting.

Skipper puffed out his chest as he forked a bite. "Can't complain about the day. Cake like this makes it perfect."

The knock at the door was sharp, cutting through the hum of conversation in the kitchen. Doris started toward it, towel in her hands.

"I'll get it," Ben said, rising. "You've done enough tonight."

He opened the door — and froze.

* * *

It took a moment for his brain to catch up with what he was seeing.

Tuesday. Here.

She stepped inside without hesitation, her gaze sharp.

“Who is it, Ben?” Doris called, coming into the hall—then stopping short at the sight of a woman dressed head to toe in black.

Tuesday didn’t wait.

“I’ve been watching Paul Ellsworth.”

* * *

“Perhaps we all better sit down.” Doris led the way back into the living room.

Fiona blinked, stunned. "Tuesday?"

Rich nearly dropped his mug. "What the hell—"

Maya jumped to her feet, eyes wide.

Thomas rose to his feet, voice hard. "What business do you have here?"

Ben rushed to explain. “Tuesday is a family friend. She’s—here about—Ellsworth.” He turned to Tuesday, waiting for her to jump in.

"How long have you been watching him?" Ben asked.

"Long enough."

“The boat he’s using—*The Alibi*—slipped into Vallejo tonight,” she continued.

Ben shook his head. "If Ellsworth's here—"

Maya was already moving. “We should let my dad’s attorney know too. I left my laptop in the car—I’ll grab it.”

Harper stood, all six foot two inches of him tense, eyes narrowing on Tuesday. "And we're supposed to take your word for it?"

Tuesday didn't flinch. "I’ve had him on my radar.”

Before anyone could press further, Rich's expression shifted. He glanced toward the kitchen window, then the empty chair where Maya had been.

* * *

She pulled on her sweater and slippers and stepped out onto the porch. The light above buzzed faintly in the cool night. Across the yard, the car waited, quiet under the glow of the streetlamp.

She crossed to it, keys in hand, already picturing the bag in the trunk.

Maya lifted the trunk.

The night was quiet.

Then a shadow moved.

A rough hand clamped over her mouth, the sharp sting of chemical fumes flooding her nose. Maya thrashed, her muffled cry smothered against the cloth. Her keys scattered across the driveway, glinting once under the porch light before vanishing into the dark.

Her strength faltered fast. Her limbs turning heavy.

The van door slid open with a metallic slam. She was hauled inside. The door slammed shut with a final crash.

By the time the vehicle sped off into the night, Maya's struggles had already gone slack.

* * *

Rich's stomach dropped, cold and sudden. It was taking too long. "She went out to the car," he muttered, already moving.

He tore the front door open, shouting into the dark. "Maya! Maya!"

Silence.

He ran to the driveway. The trunk gaped open, one slipper kicked loose on the pavement. No Maya.

Rich's heart slammed. "No. No, no, no—" He sprinted back inside, his face ashen, his voice breaking.

"She's gone."

Tuesday didn't move. But something in her eyes hardened.

"They've got her."

The room fell silent except for Doris's gasp.

The cake knife clattered against the plate.

* * *

When the blindfold came off, the air smelled of salt and diesel. The deck shifted beneath her bare feet, water lapping against the hull. Maya blinked into the dim light. She was on a boat, her wrists bound behind her.

And there they were.

Mallory leaned against the cabin wall, arms folded, her green eyes like steel. Beside her, Paul stood in filthy trousers and stained shoes, the stink of the elephant pen still clinging to him.

Paul looked away, jaw tight, unable to meet Maya's eyes.

"This is a nightmare," Maya whispered.

"No, darling," Mallory said, her voice soft and cruel. "This is the bill coming due."

CHAPTER THIRTY-NINE

SOS

* * *

SOS — a universal distress signal requesting immediate assistance.

* * *

The yacht's engines rumbled low as it slipped from port, its lights kept dark as Vallejo's shoreline faded behind.

The Alibi cut into the Bay, black water slapping hard against its hull. The cabin smelled of diesel and salt, each roll of the waves sending it creaking deeper into the night.

Maya sat bound to a bench, wrists raw against the rope, her heart hammering in time with the throb of the engines.

Mallory paced before her, sneakers whispering on the boards, eyes burning in the swinging cabin light.

"You couldn't leave it alone, could you? You had to dig, to meddle, to stick your nose into business that wasn't yours. First the club. Then your father. Then the records. You never stopped. Look at the mess you've made. My networks, my clients, my entire operation—ash. All because of you."

Maya lifted her chin, defiance cutting through fear. "You came after my father. You brought this on yourself."

Mallory's face twisted, then smoothed into cold dismissal. "Don't flatter yourself. That was Paul."

Paul flinched in the corner, eyes downcast.

"Tell her," Mallory barked.

He shook his head. "I don't want to."

"Tell her!" Mallory snapped, her fury echoing off the steel.

Maya's eyes blazed. "It doesn't matter which of you started it. Greed was your downfall. You thought you could bleed the city dry and no one would stand in your way. You were wrong."

Mallory leaned close, her breath sharp against Maya's cheek. "You talk like you're some kind of avenger. But you're nothing. And you're going to get exactly what you deserve."

The yacht bucked hard, spray rattling against the cabin windows. The light swung overhead, casting long shadows across the ropes cutting into Maya's wrists.

Mallory prowled the cabin like a caged animal, her sneakers whispering against the boards. Her eyes gleamed.

"You think you're clever. You and your little friends cost me everything."

Maya studied them, her pulse racing. She'd seen it before, the dynamic between them. Mallory the predator. Paul something smaller. He wasn't innocent, but he wasn't the monster in the room. Weak, selfish, complicit, but not psychotic. That belonged to Mallory.

The yacht pitched hard as a gust shoved against it, the Bay rough under night winds. Water slammed the hull in heavy rhythm, the cabin shuddering with each wave.

Maya thought of her grandfather's flags, the lessons long ago on the Vallejo shore. She clenched her hands, searching for anything—a cloth, a signal.

Through the porthole, faint lights glimmered ahead. The island.

CHAPTER FORTY

Mayday

* * *

MAYDAY — an international distress signal indicating imminent danger.

* * *

Tuesday's voice cut through the tension, flat and sure. "If they've taken Maya, they'll be headed toward San Francisco now. Treasure Island. That's where I'd start."

"Treasure Island?" Fiona asked, pulling her jacket tighter.

"Why there?" Ben pressed.

Skipper's eyes shifted from the window. "It used to be a Naval Station. Shut down now. Remote, but close to both shores. Easy place to hide something you don't want found."

Tuesday nodded once.

Thomas stopped pacing. "Then we don't waste time. I'll call in a favor. I know a man with a boat down at the marina. He'll get us out on the Bay fast."

Fiona snatched her keys from the counter. "I'll take the freeway. It's the fastest way across. Tuesday, you're with me."

Doris straightened, her face pained but determined. "That's my daughter out there. I'm not staying behind."

Ben's voice broke through, calm but firm. "And the Coast Guard?"

All eyes turned to him.

"We'll handle that," Rich said "You're with me."

Skipper finally spoke, his voice steady as iron. "We split up, we move fast, and we don't stop until we have her back."

The Bay opened wide before them, dark waves flashing white under the moon. Thomas gripped the wheel of the borrowed boat, his jaw locked.

"She's out there. You can feel it," Skipper said, braced against the rail. His old instincts flared alive. "Treasure Island. Always was a Navy hideout. Now it's empty space."

Thomas nodded. "Then we catch her before she slips past." He throttled forward, spray misting across their faces as the engine roared.

Fiona's jeep barreled west, headlights cutting the night. Doris clutched the dashboard. Tuesday leaned forward between the seats, scanning the road.

"Treasure Island's the funnel," Tuesday said. "If they dock, we'll be waiting."

Doris's voice trembled but held. "We'll get her back. We just have to."

Fiona pressed the accelerator. "We will."

Ben leaned over the desk, his voice even but urgent. "A vessel left Vallejo. The Alibi. They've taken Maya Forrester."

The duty officer frowned, skeptical. "That's a serious claim."

Rich slammed his palms down. "She's my girl, and she's out there right now! You've got cutters, you've got radar — use them!"

Ben steadied his friend with a hand. "Please. The kidnappers may be Paul Ellsworth and Mallory Thornton."

The officer finally reached for the radio. "We'll make the call."

The hunt for The Alibi was on.

CHAPTER FORTY-ONE

The Deepest Hold

* * *

DEEPEST HOLD — the lowest cargo compartment of a vessel.

* * *

The night wind tore at Paul Ellsworth's clothes as he crouched low on the forward deck, the yacht bucking beneath him, salt stinging his lips, the roar of the Bay filling his ears.

He wanted to leap. Every muscle in him screamed 'abandon ship', to disappear into the dark water and let the tide take him anywhere but here.

But he couldn't. Not yet.

Maya Forrester was below deck with his sister, bound and helpless. And though Paul hadn't laid a hand on her, he knew he was complicit. His silence, his cowardice, his hunger for leverage had placed her in Mallory's grasp.

The weight of his life pressed in on him. He saw his childhood, Mallory towering over him like a sentence he had never escaped. He saw Marty Butler in the basement room—his own prisoner. It all crowded him now, crashing in from every side.

His sister was unraveling. He could see it in her eyes, hear it in the venom of her voice. Mallory Thornton had nothing left to lose — and that made her deadly.

And Maya? Maya was a victim caught in the storm.

Paul gripped the rail, his hands trembling. He could run. He could leap now and vanish, let the Bay swallow him, and hope that the current carried him somewhere Mallory would never find him.

But the thought of Maya left behind, alone with his sister's rage, curdled in his gut.

If he was going to sever the chain Mallory had looped around his neck since childhood, he would have to end her hold on him.

Not killing her. No, Paul was never built for that.

But turning against her.

Helping Maya was the only way out. Survival, yes — but also the first choice in years that was his own, not Mallory's.

Paul drew a breath, the decision settled heavy in his chest. Somewhere in the dark, a plan began to form—jagged, desperate, but his.

When Mallory turned to the pilot, jabbing her finger at the charts, Paul moved. He slipped from the cabin, reappeared moments later with something in his hand.

A knife.

Maya's chest seized. For an instant she braced, heart hammering, certain he meant to silence her before his sister snapped.

But Paul crouched, the knife glinting in his palm. He didn't come at her blade-first — he turned the handle toward her first. His eyes met hers, wide, urgent.

Maya stilled. Her instincts screamed not to trust him. But her mind moved faster than fear. Mallory was the threat. Paul was desperate. Desperate people turned when survival demanded it.

Paul leaned closer, pressing the blade under the ropes. With a quick slice, the fibers loosened. Before pulling back, he slipped the knife into her hand, hidden by her sleeve.

Their eyes locked. An unspoken truth passed between them: for this moment, they were allies.

Maya's fingers tightened on the handle. She didn't lash out — not yet. She forced herself to stay cool, to stay small, to let Mallory believe she was still bound. Because survival meant timing.

Mallory's voice cut back across the cabin. "Faster! I want her on that dock before dawn. I want her to see where she's going to disappear."

Maya lowered her gaze, heart pounding. The ropes hung slack around her wrists. The knife was warm in her hand. She had what she needed.

CHAPTER FORTY-TWO

Treasure Island

* * *

TREASURE ISLAND — a man-made island in the San Francisco Bay.

* * *

Fiona's jeep wove through freeway traffic like it was born for it, headlights streaking past as horns chased in her wake. Doris clutched the door handle and pressed both feet firmly into the floorboard.

Tuesday, leaning forward between the seats, kept her eyes on the road.

Fiona's focus snapped to the overhead sign flashing green: **EXIT 4 – Treasure Island / Yerba Buena – LEFT EXIT.**

Her gut dropped. She was running too far right.

"Damn it!" Fiona snarled, yanking the wheel. The jeep lunged across lanes, horns blaring, high beams flashing as drivers braked and swerved to avoid her. Doris gasped, bracing herself against the dash. Tires squealed as Fiona forced the jeep into the narrowing left-hand ramp, threading the needle at the last possible instant.

Tuesday let out a dry laugh, shaking her head. "This feels familiar."

Fiona shot her a look in the rearview mirror but didn't answer. Doris just gripped the dash tighter. "Fiona!" she admonished. "You're going to get us killed!"

The ramp curved down toward the water, Treasure Island waiting like a shadow between the bridges.

The freeway ramp spilled the jeep onto the island. Fiona downshifted, tires squealing as she took the curve hard. Treasure Island loomed ahead in shadows and sodium light — old Navy buildings shuttered, chain-link fences sagging, streetlamps buzzing like dying fireflies.

Doris gripped the dash with both hands, her breath quick.

Tuesday's eyes swept the darkness. "Not empty tonight."

They rounded a bend and there it was: The Alibi, tied off at a battered pier, its hull rocking gently against the pilings. A single figure moved on deck, shadow cutting across the weak light.

Fiona killed the headlights and rolled them into the cover of a derelict warehouse. She shut off the engine, silence falling hard.

"Now what?" Doris whispered.

"Now we wait," Tuesday said, scanning. "We're not alone."

Out on the water, Thomas's borrowed boat cut through the chop, Skipper braced at the bow. His hand lifted, pointing. "There! At the pier. That's her."

Thomas throttled forward, spray lashing his face. "We'll be on her in minutes."

The helicopter shuddered in the crosswind, rotors thundering over the surf. Ben gripped the seat frame with both hands, knuckles white under the straps across his chest. He kept his head down, every sway of the craft threatening to turn his stomach.

Across from him, Rich leaned toward the window, eyes locked on the dark water below. He wasn't afraid. He was beyond that now, fixed only on the yacht below.

"There," Rich said hoarsely, jabbing a finger at the glass. "That's her. That's The Alibi."

“Visual confirmed,” the pilot said over the intercom. “Vessel tied at the pier. One figure on deck.”

The pilot banked, the helicopter circling lower. "We'll hold pattern. Ground and water units should be closing."

"Copy," the crewman said. "Searchlight ready on your mark."

Ben closed his eyes for a moment, gripping harder as the cabin rattled. Rich pressed closer to the glass, never blinking.

"Hang on, Maya," Rich muttered. "We're here."

The crewman flicked the switch. The searchlight snapped on, a brilliant cone stabbing down onto the pier, catching The Alibi in its glare.

On deck, Mallory's voice cracked through the night like a whip. "Forget it — let’s go! Take her around the island. Lose the light."

The pilot jumped back on board and gunned the throttle, and The Alibi tore free from the dock, cutting a hard line into the black water. The Coast Guard's searchlight swept after it, bouncing across the waves.

With the knife hidden in her sleeve, Maya staggered upright as the yacht pitched. Her lungs burned. Her heart screamed one word: Run.

She stumbled for the rail, preparing to leap for open water—

Mallory's hand clamped in her hair, yanking her back hard. "Not so easy, darling."

Maya's cry split the night. The knife slipped, clattering across the deck. The yacht heaved again, the waves rough and unforgiving.

Paul lunged. He tore Mallory off, grappling her across the swaying boards. "Enough, Mallory!" His voice broke with rage and desperation.

They fell into a tangle, brother and sister, fists and elbows striking out.

A loose cloth snapped near the rail. Maya grabbed it and ripped it in two.

The pilot shouted from the wheel. "Hold on, we're swinging wide!"

Spray lashed across the bow as their borrowed boat pounded through the chop. Skipper squinted through the dark, his eyes catching frantic movement on The Alibi's stern. Then he froze.

Two pale shapes—Maya's arms, whipping a torn strip of cloth in deliberate motions.

Semaphore.

He caught the rhythm instantly, the old patterns drilled decades ago.

"H-E-L-P," he breathed. Then louder: "That's her! That's my girl!"

Thomas leaned hard on the throttle, the boat roaring toward the island.

Rich cupped his hands to the window, using them as makeshift binoculars, his fists hammering against the frame. "She's signaling! She's alive!"

Ben forced his eyes open, following his friend's point, and saw it too — jerky but purposeful, the cloth rising and falling. His stomach turned, but his chest swelled.

The crewman called it in: "Visual confirmation. Distress signal from target vessel."

The pilot's voice was taut. "They're losing control. Hold position."

The struggle between Mallory and Paul slammed into the helm.

The pilot cursed, yanking at the controls. Too late.

The yacht slammed against the rocks, its hull screaming as water poured in. The deck pitched violently, sending crates and glass crashing across the cabin.

Maya staggered to her feet and picked up the knife. It was slick in her grip, but Mallory was already on her, shoving her hard against the rail.

The pilot bolted, dragging the only life raft free. He shoved it over and leapt, paddling away without a backward glance.

"You ruined everything!" Mallory's voice was ragged, eyes blazing. "All of it—gone because of you!"

Paul lunged between them, arms locking around his sister's shoulders. "Stop, Mallory! It's over!"

She shrieked, twisting, clawing at him like a wild thing. "You were mine, Paul! Mine to command!"

The deck pitched, water flooding fast. Maya scrambled toward the open air, but she looked back—just once—and saw Paul holding his sister, his face crumpling.

"I'm sorry," he whispered—not to Mallory, not to Maya, maybe not even to himself. Just a raw sound, torn from his chest.

Then the rail gave way, and the siblings tumbled into the dark, their struggle swallowed by the Bay.

Water surged across the deck, cold and black, dragging Maya toward the rail. She kicked free of the ropes, the knife still clutched in her hand, but the flood pressed her down.

The pilot's raft bobbed away into the night.

The Alibi was going down.

Maya's head broke the surface as she gasped for air — then she slipped under again, water filling her nose and throat.

Fiona's jeep screeched to a halt at the edge of the ruined pier. They tumbled out, Doris's cry carrying over the water as the yacht's bow dipped.

"There!" Doris screamed, pointing. "Maya!"

Tuesday steadied her, eyes darting from the wreck to the pursuing boats and the helicopter overhead. "They're on her. We just have to be ready when she makes shore."

Fiona cupped her hands, shouting across the surf. "Hold on, Maya!"

Thomas steered hard, their borrowed boat skimming close, the searchlight cutting across the wreck. His eyes locked on the figure thrashing in the black water.

His chest seized. "Maya—"

Before he could angle the bow closer, a splash cracked behind him. Thomas spun. Skipper's track suit was already vanishing into the dark, arms slicing through the chop with surprising strength.

"Go, Harp," Thomas muttered through clenched teeth, shoving the throttle forward to shadow them in. Spray slapped across his face, but he never took his eyes off the two figures in the water — one sinking, one charging straight for her.

The Alibi's bow pitched, metal shrieking as it tore along the rocks. Maya's fingers slipped from the slick rail. The next wave dragged her under.

From above, the helicopter's searchlight locked on Maya as she slipped under again.

Rich tore at his harness, shouting over the comms. "Drop me! I'll go down!"

The crewman shoved him back into his seat. "Negative! You're not qualified for a wet hoist."

The pilot's voice was steady. "Stand by. Recovery in progress."

Ben gripped Rich's arm, holding him down. "She's not alone. Look — Skipper's in the water."

Then an arm locked around her chest, hauling her upward. She gasped, coughing salt and diesel, blinking into the spray.

"Got you," Skipper growled, his grip steady as iron.

He kicked hard, pulling her clear of the wreckage as Thomas swung the borrowed boat close. Thomas reached down with both arms, hauling Maya aboard, dripping and trembling, her hair plastered across her face.

Thomas wrapped Maya in his coat, his voice breaking. "You're safe now. You're safe."

Skipper scrambled up next, coughing but grinning, his chest heaving with effort.

Behind them, The Alibi groaned and slipped beneath the water, dragging Mallory and Paul with it. Their shouts were swallowed by the waves. The pilot's life raft bobbed farther out, but no one cared.

Tuesday scanned the shadows, keeping watch, but Doris didn't care — her eyes were only on the boat closing in. Doris called Maya's name.

Thomas and Skipper steadied Maya as they guided her across the slick deck. When the bow kissed the dock, Doris was there, clutching her daughter so tightly Maya could barely breathe.

"Maya—" Doris's voice broke. She kissed Maya's forehead. "You're here. You're here."

Maya's body shook with exhaustion, but she smiled faintly. "Mom, I'm okay."

The Coast Guard chopper touched down on the far end of the pier, rotors still thrumming. Rich was out before the skids settled, sprinting down the boards. He barreled into Maya, pulling her into his arms, his voice cracking. "I thought I lost you. I thought—"

She buried her face in his chest, whispering, "You didn't. I'm here."

Ben followed at a slower pace, relief etched across his tired features. He caught Fiona's eye, then Tuesday's. They didn't speak — but the nods said everything.

The family was together again.

Behind them, the Bay swallowed the last bubbles of The Alibi, the night finally still.

Then Thomas stiffened, his eyes on the water.

A pale hand broke the surface, then a head — Paul Ellsworth, coughing and sputtering as he clung to a broken plank.

“After everything,” Thomas said roughly, “he’s still alive.”

Paul Ellsworth was hauled out of the water onto the pier. He collapsed on hands and knees, coughing, chest heaving. His eyes darted along the shadows, as if still searching for his sister.

From those same shadows, Tuesday stepped forward. The brass key at her necklace glinted in the dock lights as she crouched down beside him.

Tuesday's voice was low but carried enough for the others to hear. "It's over, Paul. She's not coming back."

Paul's breath hitched. Water dripped from his chin to the boards. For a long moment, he didn't move.

Tuesday straightened, her gaze still on him. "You're on your own now."

The words settled over the dock like a verdict. For the first time in his life, Paul Ellsworth was without Mallory. No leash. No shield. No excuses left.

His shoulders began to shake. "I'm so sorry," he sobbed.

No one answered.

The Coast Guard moved in, hauling him to his feet.

Tuesday's eyes found Maya. For a long beat, neither spoke. Then Tuesday gave a single nod—half acknowledgment, half promise.

Maya managed a faint, exhausted smile as the sirens drew closer and officers led Ellsworth down the dock.

CHAPTER FORTY-THREE

The Sounding Line

* * *

SOUNDING LINE — weighted rope to measure depth.

* * *

Three days later, the Bay glittered under a flawless sky. Fleet Week banners still flapped along the Embarcadero, jets arced overhead, and ferries thrummed between San Francisco and Oakland. Life pushed on.

At Oakland International, Skipper adjusted the strap of his overnight bag. Rich stood beside Maya at the curb, both of them sun-tired from the last days of ceremonies.

"You sure you've got everything?" Maya asked.

Skipper grinned, tugging at the collar of his track suit. "Medals in the bag. Coffee in my veins. That's all a man needs."

Rich hugged him hard. "Safe flight, Skipper."

Maya kissed his cheek. "See you soon, Grandpa."

He lifted a hand in salute before disappearing through the sliding doors, swallowed by the crowd.

* * *

On the waterfront, Thomas leaned against the railing of a gantry crane. Containers swung steadily in their harnesses, longshore workers calling out in practiced rhythm. The port was alive again, labor humming where silence had nearly taken root.

He drew a deep breath of salt air. Below him, cranes swung containers through the sky with the slow rhythm of a heartbeat.

* * *

In downtown Oakland, campaign posters lined windows and telephone poles. Vote Ben Cooper sprouted on lawns, cafés, and storefronts. Ben moved from one handshake to the next, voice steady, suit rumpled from long days.

Fiona was never far, her clipboard snapping shut as she barked reminders to volunteers. "Don't let them walk away without registering. The election is in two weeks. Every single vote counts."

The energy around them had shifted. The city wasn't just listening anymore — it was leaning forward.

* * *

Paul Ellsworth didn't see any of it.

He sat behind bars at Santa Rita once again, this time under a stack of new charges: kidnapping, larceny, conspiracy. Any chance of parole was gone. The man who once imagined himself untouchable now stared at cinderblock walls and steel bars, his sister gone.

* * *

Key & Cup was quiet that afternoon, sunlight slanting through the windows and catching the steam from Tuesday's mug. She sat across from Wallace.

Wallace leaned back in his chair, a smile creasing his weathered face. "Feels different now, doesn't it? City's stirring. Ben's campaign — the way folks are talking about change again."

Tuesday sipped her tea, her expression calm but her eyes sharp. "Things can turn fast. A few weeks ago it felt like the Bay was breaking apart. Now everyone's talking about building again."

"Proud of that boy," Wallace said.

"Like father, like son." Tuesday offered.

Wallace looked around at the hum of activity.

"Benjamin and his friends have come a long way since the night you arrived at my garage."

Tuesday's smile widened, small but real. "They have."

She set her mug down and stood, pulling her coat tight.

"Heading out?" Wallace asked.

Tuesday nodded. "For now."

He studied her a moment, his hand resting on the table. "Will I see you again?"

Tuesday's eyes softened, but she gave no answer.

She slipped her hands into her pockets and walked toward the door.

The bell chimed softly as she stepped into the light.

EPILOGUE

Safe Harbor

* * *

SAFE HARBOR — protected anchorage where vessels find shelter from storms.

* * *

Key & Cup – Election night

Every table was covered with pizza boxes, paper cups, or campaign flyers. The crowd thrummed with energy. The television mounted above the counter blared returns, the volume rising with each county update. Volunteers packed shoulder to shoulder, their voices swelling with nervous laughter and bursts of applause as numbers rolled in.

At the center of it all, Ben stood with Fiona at his side, both looking tired but electric, their hands clasped tight.

Maya slipped away from the noise, stepping out onto the small back patio with Rich. The air was cool, the muffled roar of the crowd still leaking through the walls.

"I keep thinking about everything," she said softly. "The spreadsheets, the reports, the day-to-day grind. It's not enough anymore. Not after this."

Rich slid his arm around her shoulders. "Not enough how?"

She looked up at him, her eyes bright.

"When I helped Dad prove his innocence... I felt useful. Like I was actually doing something that mattered.

Marty Butler's in protective custody. He's going to testify. People like Ellsworth—they need to be held accountable. But more than that, they need to be stopped before they can do so much harm. I don't want to just analyze problems. I want to solve them."

Rich's brow furrowed. "Solve them how?"

"I'm going to apply to law school," Maya said. Her voice grew steadier with each word. "And one day, I'm going to sit on the bench as a judge."

For a moment, Rich just stared at her. Then his face broke into a wide, unguarded smile. He pulled her closer, pressing a kiss to her temple. "I love you, Maya Forrester. And I want you to have everything you're reaching for. If this is it, then you go after it with everything you've got."

She smiled into his chest, her heartbeat calm for the first time in weeks.

The roar inside the café swelled, the anchor's voice rising over the feed: "In a sweeping come-from-behind victory, we're now able to make a projection in Oakland's District Four council race. With ninety-five percent of precincts reporting, we can call this race for Benjamin Cooper, at just twenty-five years old, the youngest city councilmember ever elected in Oakland."

The room erupted. Chairs scraped, hands clapped, shouts shook the walls. Ben swept Fiona into his arms, spinning her in a circle before planting a kiss on her lips. Volunteers cheered, cameras flashed, and chants of "Coo-per! Coo-per!" filled the night.

On the patio, Maya and Rich leaned together, smiling through the noise. The future didn't feel uncertain—it felt wide open, like the water stretching beyond the harbor.

* * *

Author's Note

The idea for setting this story at the Port of Oakland came from spending time around the waterfront and realizing how much of a city's life happens just out of sight.

From a distance, the cranes that line the harbor look almost like part of the skyline, giant shapes moving slowly against the bay. But anyone who spends time near the port understands those machines are only the surface of something much larger. What really drives the place are the people who show up every day to work there and the communities that have grown up around it.

For generations, longshore workers, truck drivers, warehouse crews, and countless others have kept the port moving. Their schedules shape the rhythm of the waterfront, ships arriving before dawn, containers shifting across the yards, trucks rolling out toward the rest of the Bay Area. It's demanding work, and much of it happens without fanfare, even though it quietly supports the daily life of the entire region.

Oakland has always been a port city, and that reality has helped shape the character of the East Bay in ways both visible and subtle. The waterfront is where global commerce meets local neighborhoods, where families build careers, and where the fortunes of the city can rise or stall with the movement of a single ship.

The story in this book is fictional, but the setting is very real. The plot imagines pressures and conflicts pushed to their limits, but the world it unfolds in is drawn from a place where people show up every day to do work that keeps the city moving.

If nothing else, I hope the story leaves readers with a slightly different perspective the next time they see those cranes rising over the water.

Stories like this are imagined, but the forces that shape them are not.

Acknowledgements

Every novel is shaped by more people than the author whose name appears on the cover.

I'm grateful to the friends and family who encouraged the long process of turning an idea into a finished book and a finished book into a series.

My thanks to the early readers who offered thoughtful reactions to the manuscript and to the spirit of the story.

Any remaining errors, or overly imaginative leaps, are mine alone

Also by Parker Daugherty

Brass Secrets

Hall of Frame

Past & Perfect

Discussion Guide

Harbor Code explores the systems that shape a city: ports, labor, redevelopment, loyalty, silence, and the hidden structures that determine who carries the weight when those systems begin to fail. Beneath the mystery and investigation is a story about pressure, institutional pressure, personal pressure, inherited pressure, and the choices people make while trying to survive inside it.

These questions are intended to encourage conversation, reflection, and interpretation. Follow the threads that resonate most with your group.

* * *

I. THE PORT, THE CITY, AND THE WORK

The Port of Oakland is not simply a setting. It is a world governed by schedules, manifests, machinery, contracts, and unwritten rules. Labor here is identity, history, and inheritance. The novel takes that world seriously, and the questions it asks about power and accountability begin on the docks.

1.

Thomas Forrester has spent years learning how to move through the rhythms and dangers of the port. How does the novel portray dock work as more than employment? In what ways does labor become identity, responsibility, and community?

2.

The port functions almost like its own living system throughout the novel, governed by schedules, manifests, machinery, contracts, and unwritten rules. Which parts of that system feel stable, and which parts feel fragile beneath the surface?

3.

The novel repeatedly contrasts public narratives with private realities. How do official stories differ from what characters actually experience inside institutions like the port, the city, and law enforcement?

4.

Redevelopment and economic pressure remain present in the background of Harbor Code. How does the changing waterfront mirror larger questions about who gets protected, who gets displaced, and who gets forgotten?

* * *

II. POWER, ACCOUNTABILITY, AND THE DISTANCE BETWEEN THEM

The novel avoids presenting power as simple or singular. Mallory, Ellsworth, city institutions, labor systems, and financial interests all operate differently, and none of them operates openly. The most dangerous power in the novel is the kind that leaves no paper trail.

5.

Paul Ellsworth spends much of the novel trying to maintain control while quietly realizing how much control he may already have lost. What moments reveal the gap between authority and actual security?

6.

Harbor Code avoids presenting power as simple or singular. Mallory, Ellsworth, city institutions, labor systems, and financial interests all operate differently. Which form of power in the novel feels most dangerous, and why?

7.

Several characters justify morally questionable choices by framing them as necessary, practical, or inevitable. At what point does justification become excuse? Did your opinion of any character shift as the novel progressed?

8.

Mallory often believes he understands people because he understands leverage. What blind spots does that create for him throughout the story?

* * *

III. CHARACTERS AT THE EDGE OF THEMSELVES

The most interesting moments in Harbor Code are not the confrontations but the realizations: the moment a character understands the scale of what they have stepped into, or recognizes that the system they trusted has been working against them all along.

9.

Maya begins the novel searching for answers about her father, but over time her role becomes much larger than investigation alone. What internal changes occur in Maya as she realizes the scale of what she has stepped into?

10.

Paul Ellsworth is not presented as a traditional villain. The novel allows moments where he recognizes the systems surrounding him may no longer protect him. Did this change how you viewed him? Why or why not?

11.

Clare Hinton's instincts often place her slightly ahead of the official narrative. What drives her persistence? Do you see her primarily as an investigator, an observer, or something more personal?

12.

Several characters spend much of the novel feeling trapped inside systems larger than themselves. A cargo container. A holding cell. A waterfront contract. A political structure. An inherited obligation. How does the novel explore different forms of containment, both physical and emotional?

13.

Harbor Code quietly continues the evolving relationships between Ben, Rich, Maya, and Fiona. What does the group make possible together that none of them could manage alone? How does their trust continue to evolve after the events of Brass Secrets?

* * *

IV. WHAT THE NOVEL CARRIES

Oakland is deeply present throughout Harbor Code, not simply as setting, but as memory, economy, labor system, and emotional geography. The city shapes what the characters want, what they fear losing, and what they are willing to do to protect it.

14.

Throughout the novel, characters struggle with the difference between loyalty and silence. When does protecting someone become harmful? When does speaking become necessary?

15.

The city itself feels deeply present throughout Harbor Code, not simply as setting, but as memory, economy, labor system, and emotional geography. How does Oakland shape the choices the characters make?

16.

Harbor Code repeatedly asks whether systems built to preserve order eventually begin preserving themselves instead. Where do you see this tension operating most clearly in the novel?

17.

Many of the novel's turning points happen quietly: a hesitation, a realization, a withheld truth, a conversation that changes meaning in retrospect. Which quiet moment in the novel stayed with you the longest?

* * *

V. AFTER THE LAST PAGE

The novel ends without fully resolving every question it opens. That is not an oversight. Some of what Harbor Code carries is meant to travel forward into the next book, and into the reader.

18.

By the end of Harbor Code, several characters have gained knowledge they cannot easily set aside. What responsibility comes with seeing how systems actually operate beneath the surface?

19.

What do you think the novel ultimately believes about cities and the people trying to protect them? Is Harbor Code hopeful, cautionary, unresolved, or all three at once?

20.

If Brass Secrets explores inheritance and memory, Harbor Code explores systems and pressure. What emotional or thematic questions do you feel remain unresolved moving forward in the Talk of The Town series?

Oakland is still moving.

The harbor is still working.

The systems are still running beneath the surface.

And the work of understanding them is never entirely finished.

Parker Daugherty

Underfoot Press · Talk of The Town Series

Continue the Series

The Talk of The Town series continues in the next novel, Hall of Frame.

Each book follows the lives of the Core Four, Ben, Rich, Maya, and Fiona, exploring the systems, communities, and relationships that shape their world.

Across the series, the characters confront questions of heritage, legacy, accountability, and stewardship as their personal choices intersect with the institutions that define Oakland life.

To learn more about the series or future books, visit: underfootpress.com.

Preview of the Next Talk of The Town Novel

Hall of Frame

Chapter One

Miami International Airport was its own kind of city—fluorescent, humming, impatient. Overhead announcements collided with the scrape of rolling suitcases and the sharp hiss of espresso machines working overtime.

Rich Ortega sagged into a molded plastic chair near Gate D42, his camera bag digging into his shoulder and his shirt clung slightly from the humidity. He'd been awake for... he didn't know how long.

It had been a long week of filming in Nassau. The parades were all-night affairs. Rich and his crew filmed around the clock.

Too much sun. Too little sleep.

The last shot he'd reviewed still hovered in his mind: Junkanoo dancers exploding down Bay Street in a riot of feathers and brass and color, the beat of the goatskin drums shuddering straight into his sternum. The Spirit of Junkanoo. A short cultural documentary about the Bahamian winter festival's roots in joy, resistance, and community.

Beautiful, demanding work.

And now it was behind him.

He was headed back to California, Oakland specifically, not for rest, but because his sister Leela had sent three increasingly worried texts about their mother's health.

He sipped cold airport coffee and let the exhaustion drag at him.

His phone buzzed in his hand. Unknown number.

"Yeah," he answered, voice rough.

"Mr. Ortega? Caleb Ross, producer with KQSF. We're launching a new documentary on Bay Area landmarks—legacy projects that shaped civic identity. We'd like you to front the feature on the Oakland Coliseum. Specifically, the Mount Davis expansion. The story behind the story."

Rich blinked at the crowded terminal as if the world had tilted.

"That was—what? 1995?" he said. "Ninety-six?"

"Exactly!" Caleb replied. "You're from Oakland. You know what it meant when the Raiders came back from Los Angeles. We want that hometown gravitas. Nostalgia, civic pride. You'd be the perfect voice."

Perfect.

The word burrowed under his sternum, heavy and unwelcome.

He gave the noncommittal professional answer—"I'll think about it"—and ended the call.

Above him, the muted television in the bar replayed archival shots of the Oakland Coliseum.

The chyron read:

OAKLAND RAIDERS NEGOTIATIONS STALL — VEGAS DEAL CLOSING IN.

The upper deck looked hollow in the morning light. A monument to ambition. Or to denial, graying concrete slabs, lacking the grandeur that was promised

His phone buzzed again.

Leela. Fifth missed call.

He answered.

No greeting was how his sister showed urgency.

"Mom was at the hospital again today Rich," she said. "She's home now. They gave her a breathing treatment. We need you here. Sooner rather than later. I can't keep up with all of this by myself."

He exhaled, looking up at the departure board.

OAK → DELAYED New departure: 11:52 PM

"I'm coming," he said quietly. His voice didn't sound like his. "See you tomorrow."

The redeye was a blur of turbulence and half-sleep. "Good morning, ladies and gentlemen. We are now on our final approach into Oakland International Airport. Please ensure your seat backs and tray tables are in their full upright and locked position, your seat belt is securely fastened, and all carry-on items are properly stowed. We will be landing shortly."

The flight attendants were busily collecting trash and distributing instructions to waking passengers.

When the plane touched down, morning fog draped over Oakland like a damp veil. The hills were faint silhouettes.

Rich felt the old familiarity rise in him—comfort and ache, intertwined.

Outside, the air smelled the same as always: eucalyptus, diesel fumes, damp concrete, and something metallic he could never quite name.

He rented a spacious Grand Cherokee and headed up Hegenberger Road onto the highway headed North on Interstate 880.

Traffic was light. He was seeing the sign for the Oakland-Alameda County Coliseum come into view.

Then, like a memory come to life, he could see his father behind the steering wheel, he and his brothers arguing in the back seat over who got to hold the tickets, the smell of barbecues drifting in from the tailgates.

His mind replayed the many games, won and lost and all the snacks and laughs they shared as a family.

He also reflected on the times he and his best friend took the bus out to see the Oakland A's play in the summers. They sat in the bleachers, hoping to catch foul balls.

That world that felt impossibly far away now as he put Oakland in the rearview mirror and headed to Berkeley with the hope that he could check in early to his hotel room.

The hotel was quiet at this time. Gulls cried somewhere out on the water, their voices thin and distant. From his balcony, the bay stretched wide, a sheet of silver shifting under the fog.

He inhaled slowly.

He could still picture it: a park bench at the end of the pier holding Maya in his arms. He thought promises would hold them forever.

Forever had turned out to be shorter than he'd imagined.

Rich's phone buzzed, vibrating across the desk.

He stepped back into the room. His phone vibrated again.

Caleb Ross.

Rich stared at the screen, his thumb hovering. For a moment, he thought about letting it ring out. He was here on family time, not business. He didn't need a new assignment.

Instead, he drew in a breath and answered.

Made in the USA
Monee, IL
13 June 2026

54071472R00144